CHASING THE SHADOWS

TORI MARTIN

PROLOGUE

The windowpane whispers softly as I slide it up. A floorboard creaks beneath my feet, and my eyes dart towards the five-year-old girl in the bottom bunk. But I needn't have worried; a passing freight train wouldn't wake Lula up.

I take a final, sweeping glance around the room before letting my duffel bag slip from my fingers and into the flowerbed below. I ease myself out of the window and onto a sturdy oak branch. I almost laugh. This is too easy.

I swing down onto the trunk and scamper to the ground, retrieving my black bag from its spot among the dahlias. Mrs. Baker is going to be really happy in the morning when she sees the crushed flowers. One corner of my mouth curves up into a smile. The plump, nasty-faced woman deserves it. It's small payback for how she's treated me. I involuntarily rub the bruise on my arm, still sore from the woman's deadly grip on it last night. I didn't open that package of cookies; it was probably Lula or her older brother who did it. But since I don't belong, I'm the natural scapegoat.

A broken streetlight stares at me from across the street, it's shattered shield yawning around a mouth full of sharp teeth. I shake off the shivers slithering down my spine. I'm not afraid. I'm excited. I'm free.

AJ promised to be waiting beneath the overpass on Second Street, and I hurry toward it. There's a bitter chill in the air, and I snuggle deeper into my sweatshirt.

Glass crunches underfoot as I leave the small suburb. Broken windows and streetlights leave empty holes where light and memories were once held, an empty testimony to what could have been. Cars whiz by, briefly blinding me with yellow bursts of light. But mostly it's quiet. This part of the city is asleep.

When I reach the west side, things get a little livelier. Bass thumps from a dilapidated apartment. Little pinpoints of light mark homeless souls finding shelter wherever they can. Sweet smoke mixes with the scents of unwashed bodies and wine. I skirt a lump sprawled across the sidewalk, too drunk to make it to wherever he or she calls 'home' and focus on the overpass up ahead. I stick to the shadows. Being invisible in these places is an asset.

As I walk into the shelter of the cement fortress, a tall boy with a crop of fuzzy black hair steps toward me.

"Yo, what up, Taz?" he asks in his usual arrogant manner. AJ was born proud; he doesn't know how else to act. It's the only thing keeping him sane, though, so I don't mind.

"Nothing much," I reply with a shrug.

AJ flicks a bit of ash from the end of his cigarette and gives me a lopsided smile.

"So…the Kegs offered us a chance to make a bit of dough," he drawls after a moment. I don't ask him what this 'chance' is. AJ talks when he's ready.

"They'll pay us enough to git us out of this hick town state," he adds. "All they want us to do is stake out Rush's and take a haul out of there for 'em. Then it's Des Moines and beyond, baby."

I lean against one of the cold, grey pillars and think about it. The Kegs are one of the more organized teen gangs in the area. They'll keep their side of the bargain because AJ has done them some favours.

Rush's Jewelry Store is a small shop that specializes in fancy gems and family heirlooms- the expensive stuff. It's owned by an old man and his wife, the trusting kind, so security shouldn't be too tight around there. AJ can dismantle an alarm faster than you can say 'beep'. Together, we make a good crew.

AJ takes his time, but eventually lets me know he has already made a plan with the Kegs. I expected this. AJ contacted me yesterday to let me know that if I want out, now's my chance. Somehow, he always finds me, no matter how many states are between us. His little half brother lives with his aunt somewhere around here, though, so he comes to Ottumwa more often than most places. Not to visit his aunt- she can't stand the sight of him. She only took in Jack because he's seven and not a street hardened criminal yet. She wouldn't give AJ the time of day if he asked.

It's silently accepted that I will be his partner in crime. And I will be, because I needed a way out of the Baker's house, and it's hard to survive on the streets by yourself. I need to get out of this town. Ottumwa isn't small, but it also isn't big enough to lose yourself in for very long, either. Not like Chicago or New York City. And I need to disappear for good this time. The cops and case workers have both made it clear that the Bakers were my last chance. I've run from foster care one too many times. Unfortunately, as far as last chances go, this one sucked.

"We'll lay low until tomorrow night. I got us some food waiting down by the old shoe factory," AJ calls over his shoulder, already two steps ahead.

* * *

A small sliver of moon grins at us from the velvety expanse of the sky as we make our way toward a middle-class neighbourhood. Rush's is located in an old, renovated house near the end of the street. The surroundings are dark and quiet, unsuspecting.

I'm dressed in black from head to toe, compliments of an old dumpster behind a thrift shop. I pull an old scarf farther up my face. It stinks, but I grit my teeth and ignore it.

AJ motions me behind a tree in the backyard while he steps up on the porch. He yanks a cord I hadn't even seen, and the porch lights go out. Next, he messes with a small box in one corner before motioning me up to the back door. He lets me pick the lock. My hands are smaller and nimbler, making me faster at it even though he's picked a lot more locks than I have. A minute after we first stepped foot on the property, we're in.

Light pollution from various sources casts eerie shadows on the creamy beige walls. We're in a workshop of some kind. A wooden counter with a sink and several strange machines sits off to our left. To the right sits the huge steel hulk that harbours the most valuable of Rush's products.

"Check the front display. They might have some stuff in there, fakes and whatever all. I'll see if I can crack this safe," AJ whispers. I nod and head for the lobby.

A massive glass-fronted case runs along the far wall and around the corner toward me. A white dust sheet is thrown over it, making the room feel like a morgue. I shiver as I peel the sheet off, half expecting a dead body to be staring up at me from the case.

"Stop it, Taz," I scold myself. "This isn't a horror movie."

Rows of necklaces, boxes of sparkling rings, and piles of bracelets stretch out beneath the glass. I know these aren't real, because only an idiot would leave a solid diamond necklace in the display case overnight, but the sight still takes my breath away. Imagine having an extra couple hundred or even thousand dollars to spend for fun…

I pull my favourite tool out of my back pocket and start jimmying the lock on the case after inspecting it for any telltale alarm wires. The lock is easy to break, considering what it's protecting. I reach in and pull out a handful of glittering bracelets to stuff in my hoodie pocket.

Something creaks just outside the front door, and I freeze. The drapes are pulled, so I can't see if anyone is out there. Something scrapes in the doorknob, and a shadow dances across the large painting mounted on the wall beside the front entrance. I start easing into the back room. We aren't the only ones trying to get in this place.

"AJ!" I hiss, sliding into the back room.

"I'm almost in," he mumbles, head bent over the keypad on the safe.

"Are the Kegs coming to check on us?" I whisper.

He looks up. "Uh, no. Why would they? They know I would be highly offended if they did that."

"Someone's…" The front door creaks open, cutting off my answer.

"Let's go!" AJ whispers. He bolts for the back door. I shut it behind us as heavy footsteps clomp into the front room. We head for the trees bordering the property.

I'm halfway across the yard when a bright searchlight flicks on, illuminating us.

"Iowa State Police! Stop where you are!" a loud voice barks, sending a throb of fear shooting through my veins. I reach deep inside for an extra burst of speed, legs moving like pistons. All we have to do is make it to the trees. Beyond that, the small green space will dump us out into the slums, and we can get lost in the maze of alleys and apartments.

Ahead of me, a dark figure takes out AJ, and I veer to the left. Something hard and solid slams into me, knocking the air out of my lungs. I fall to the grass, dirt skidding under my chin. My hands are yanked behind my back. I want to rage, to scream, to curse, but nothing comes out. A heavy weight settles over my back, and cold steel bites into my wrists.

I threw away my last chance to find freedom. And I failed.

CHAPTER 1

The metal chair is freezing my thighs off. Another gust of air from the ceiling vent sends shivers down my spine. Whoever runs this place didn't worry about spending too much on air conditioning. It's only the first day of March, guys. The summer heat wave is months away.

I've been sitting in this empty room with dirty yellow walls and water stains for at least half an hour. That may not sound like a long time, but to me it feels like an eternity. I spent last night in a cell, and that wasn't much better, but at least I had a thin blanket. In here, there's nothing.

The bolt scrapes back on the door, and I sit up. A young cop walks in with a stack of papers in his hand, his green eyes narrowing as he glances my way. He sits down behind the dented gray table, tosses the sheaf of papers down, and folds his hands. I lift my chin and make sure I don't squirm. If there's one thing cops hate, it's confident troublemakers.

"I'm Officer Roydes. And you must be Anastasia?" he asks politely, even though I'm sure he knows full well who I am.

"It's Taz," I grind out through clenched teeth. Nobody is allowed to call me by my full name.

The officer raises an eyebrow. "Alright, then. Taz it is. "

He clears his throat before continuing. "The consequences were quite clear the last time you met with one of this country's fine law officers. The next time you get caught running from state care, you're headed to juvenile detention."

He doesn't have to remind me. I'm perfectly aware of the consequences of running away for the sixteenth time in nine years; I just wasn't planning to get caught.

The officer tilts back his chair and raises his eyebrows, giving me a grim stare. Finally, he leans forward, and his eyes bore into mine. I look away.

"That was supposed to be how it was going to play out. However, it appears you've gotten a little grace extended to you." His tone suggests I don't deserve what's coming next. I glare back into those hard, green eyes.

He gets up abruptly, his chair spinning back on two legs before crashing against the wall. He leans across the desk and slaps his palms down. I scoot my chair back, the metal legs screeching across the tile.

"Kate Brighton is the name of your new foster parent. Your social worker will fill you in on the details, but your charges have been waived on the condition you cooperate with your new placement and stay there. And let me tell you this- if you run away again or get yourself into any more hot water with the law, I will take great pleasure in personally signing you off to my warden friend over at Central Iowa." He hauls in a deep breath before sitting back down in his chair. He picks up the top paper and slides it across the desk toward me.

"You will have to sign this document agreeing to the following: the rules of your new foster placement, staying on the premises unless for religious or educational purposes or with the permission of your new guardian, and completing eighty hours of community service before school ends. Failure to sign this paper will send you straight to juvie. Failure to comply with the agreements outlined here will also send you to juvie, although you'll have to suffer through court proceedings first with that one. I would recommend you sign it."

He chucks a pen across the dented metal surface of the desk.

It slides off and into my lap. I pick it up and stare at the ceiling, pretending it's a hard decision.

His mouth presses into a thin line of annoyance, his expression a blank slate in an attempt to hide his rising emotions. I wait a few seconds longer, just to bug him, before grudgingly leaning forward and signing on the line. I don't bother reading the fine print- I can't change it, anyway.

"Don't make me regret this," he says, gathering the papers and standing up abruply. Then he spins on his heel and stalks out.

I sit there for a minute, processing everything. What does he have to regret? I doubt he had much sway in what my sentence would be; he barely looks old enough to be out of Police Academy.

The Bakers were my eleventh placement in Iowa. The Hawkeye State has become my home base, like it or not, even though I was born in Illinois. AJ and his extensive network of 'friends' have been my anchor, helping me escape most of the homes.

But how did they find a new placement so fast? And Kate Brighton- that's only one name. I've never been taken in by a single woman before. What would possess her to want a trouble-making teenager?

Eventually, I give up on trying to figure everything out, and stare at the watermarks and mold on the ceiling. Time drags on slower than a snail on sleeping medication, and I'm ready to go see if they've forgotten about me when I hear the click-click of stilettos coming down the hall. They stop outside the door, and I roll my eyes. My latest social worker- I've managed to push three into resigning- is the worst state employee by far. She likes children about as much as I like peanut butter on peppers- level zero.

Miss Moriah Cade enters the room and gives me a tight smile that doesn't reach her icy blue eyes. Her red lipstick is blinding, and her dress is too tight, like usual. She enjoys making my life miserable, and I don't mind returning the favour. She lets her snake-skin purse fall to her wrist and motions me out of my seat.

"Well, didn't you get into trouble," she sneers.

"Hello to you, too," I mutter back. How many snakes gave their lives for that purse? I wonder idly. Poor, innocent snakes.

"What was that? Taz, you must stop mumbling if you're to have the slightest chance that a family will want you." She wrinkles her pointy nose at me, making her look like a rat. Then, as if remembering we are in a police station with cameras all over, she gives a dry laugh and quickly adds, "Don't take that the wrong way. I'm just giving you some valuable life tips." She flashes me a smile so sugary, I start to feel a cavity form.

I roll my eyes at her back and wordlessly follow her out of the room. Moriah waves a bunch of paperwork under the receptionist's nose before leading me out to her cherry red Mini Cooper.

"I visited the Bakers this morning to give them the report. My, Mrs. Baker was in a mood. You stomped all over her prized flowers for the summer fair before you left. She wants to sue for damages. Thankfully, I was able to convince her that the legal fees would be much more than the worth of her dahlias, but why do you always have to make such a mess of things, Taz? You're nothing but trouble."

I tune Moriah out as she rambles on and on about my bad qualities, of which there are many. The city fades into acres of rolling pastures and cropland, with an occasional house or barn thrown in. In other words, it's miles of boring. I stayed at a farm once, back when I was five or six. The people that owned it were okay. They were older, and their kids had grown up and left. They gave me my own kitten from one of the many litters birthed in the old, red barn, and I had spending money every week. But of course, good things never last. The man had a stroke, and I got sent away- again. Soon after that, I started running. None of those people were going to keep me long term, anyway. Better to get out of there on my own time than have them force me to leave.

My eyes are heavy with sleep when Moriah jerks the wheel hard to the right, sending me into the door. My head cracks against the window as we career off Highway 22 onto a smaller, two-lane road.

"Oops," she chirps, swerving around a bus pulling out from a nearby station. A few minutes later, we fly by the '30 MPH' sign and enter the quiet, tree-lined streets of Oakville. It's the stereotypical all-American small town- a flag hanging from every front porch, an old stone church on every corner, and stretched over the window of a small white brick building, a pink and blue striped awning with *Pop's Soda Shop* printed on it. That's all I see of it before we're through. Moriah drives like an F-1 driver on crack. I'm surprised she isn't in jail for stunt driving yet. That would make my life a whole lot easier.

About five minutes out of town, Moriah turns down a paved laneway. It winds through a pair of stone pillars and up a hill before dumping us on the driveway of an immense, modern stone house. The house is surrounded by immaculate flower beds and ornamental trees. A row of tall oaks ring around the building, protecting it from the worst of the Iowa wind. It's an intimidating picture, at least to a kid who's never been inside a house half this size.

"I'm not staying here," I state, crossing my arms over my chest.

"Yes, you are." Moriah smiles. "Unless you'd rather sleep on a metal bunk in juvie."

Looking at this place, I almost would. I know detention centers aren't the Ritz Carlton, but this place...I'm going to wreck some priceless antique before the day ends and be sent to juvie anyway.

Moriah appears to be heartily enjoying my discomfort, so I shove my emotions aside and hop out of the Mini Cooper. I grab my duffel bag from the trunk and smile a little, remembering how it minced up Mrs. Baker's dahlias. Then I follow Moriah's blonde head up the giant stone steps to the front door.

The sound of the doorbell makes me jump, even though I'm the one who rings it. It's a deep, mellow sound that reminds me of a heartbeat. I step off to the side as the door creaks open. For once, I can put Moriah to use as a human shield.

The lady who opens the door is nothing like I expected. When I heard I was being taken in by a single woman, I was picturing some old granny, or an eccentric gardener wanting a free servant. The brunette before me can't be more than thirty-five. She's slender, beautiful, and looks like she could dash me to pieces, especially in those denim overalls. She smiles at me and introduces herself to us as 'Kate'.

Moriah nudges me harder than necessary in the ribs, and I shake the woman's hand.

"Taz," I answer.

"Or Anastasia, if you prefer," Moriah inserts. She gives me a gleeful look, and I glare back. Moriah knows how much I hate that name. "And I'm Miss Cade, but please call me Moriah."

"Come on into the kitchen, and I can sign the necessary papers," Kate invites, completely ignoring Moriah. I cheer inwardly for my new guardian and step inside. She must be catching on to Moriah's tricks. If she is, she'll be the first of my many foster parents to do so.

We follow Kate into the foyer, and I carefully wipe my shoes on the large mat. The house is open concept, with a massive stone fireplace along the one wall, and a chef's kitchen off to the left. Even the chairs at the table are stylish, with intricate carvings decorating the backrests, and I gingerly take a seat. Moriah is busy surveying the house, probably calculating dollars, so she starts when Kate sweetly asks, "The papers?"

"Oh, yes," Moriah replies hastily, flushing a little. I can tell she wants to impress such a rich lady, but I don't think she wins any points when she pulls a massive folder from her black leather briefcase.

"Alright. You'll need to sign the highlighted parts on these three papers, and then these ones, and…here, this consent form." Moriah pushes a tornado of paper Kate's way. "And if there is any trouble with Taz, don't hesitate to call me. My number is at the top of each sheet. Taz can be a bit of a…tough one sometimes, if you know what I mean. And of course, if she ever disappears, please call the authorities. We've had trouble like that in the past with this one."

My heart sinks to my toes. I don't have much hope for this place. Only three of the foster homes I've been to in my life were decent, and a record of my past activities isn't going to leave a good impression on my new host. I'm sure there are genuinely good people in the system, but I've rarely been lucky enough to stay with them. Kate surprises me by giving Moriah a cold stare and saying, "I'm sure there won't be any problems, Miss Cade."

Moriah's Cheshire cat grin turns into a pout. "I thought you might like to be forewarned," she responds feebly.

"I am aware of the situation. I don't need any reminders," Kate replies crisply, sliding the last paper Moriah's way.

Moriah glares at me as she stuffs the file back into her briefcase. As if it's my fault! I didn't say anything.

"Now, I'm sure you're busy, Miss Cade," Kate adds, "So I won't keep you. I can show Taz around the house later."

Moriah opens her mouth to protest. I'm guessing she's never been in a house this big, and she's dying to see every single room.

Kate quickly ushers the blonde social worker to the door, and slams it shut behind her. Then she turns to me, still seated at the table. I gape at her for a second before slamming my mouth shut. Who is this lady?

"How do you stand that woman?" she asks. Before I can formulate an answer, she moves on to, "Do you want to see your room?"

"Uh…s-sure," I stammer. Usually when I stay in homes, they have little kids, or at least other people in the household. From what I've seen, Kate lives all by herself in this massive house. And without chattering toddlers to break the silence, this could be a little awkward.

I follow Kate up the stairs. There's a cozy reading nook below a huge bay window at the top of the steps. I'm not a reader, but it looks like a good place to do homework, or watch a movie, or…I push the daydream out of my head. I won't be here long. I never am.

A large canvas of a smiling family dominates another wall. The young, pig-tailed girl on the woman's lap is definitely the child version of Kate. I can see her eyes in the woman, and her nose in the burly, gray-haired man sitting beside her. A tall, gangly boy stands behind his father, hands on the man's shoulders. He looks nothing like Kate, yet somehow fits into this family.

I tear my eyes away from the picture and head to my new room, which turns out to be a big space at the far end of the house. It's got a large window overlooking the backyard, framed by sheer curtains. Three of the walls are the colour of whipped cream, and the fourth one, behind the bed, is a nice sage green. A brown leather chair sits in one corner, behind a sturdy walnut desk. I let my pitiful bag of clothes slide to the floor. I feel much too dirty to be in this room. Behind me, Kate quietly leaves the room, shutting the door behind her.

I pick my bag back up and open the nearest dresser drawer. Unpacking shouldn't take too long with the amount of clothes I own. I shove a couple pairs of jeans into the top drawer and slam it shut. Visions of AJ shoving his clothes into a steel locker flit into my mind, and a twinge of guilt zips through me. Here I am, spending my seven-hundredth chance at a mansion while AJ, who is no worse than I am except for a rap sheet as long as the Declaration of Independence, is pining away behind bars.

I pull out the last of my clothes and kick my bag into a corner of the big closet.

"You're never gonna get ahead if you worry about anyone else." That's a quote straight from AJ's mouth. I push him from my thoughts.

CHAPTER 2

The sunlight streaking through the windows hurts my sleep-dazed eyes. After a quick glance at the time, I roll out of bed and plant my bare feet firmly on the floor. An uneasy feeling worms its way into my middle as I pull a T-shirt over my head. They're always nice the first day; the real Kate awaits below, already planning out how to make my life miserable and work me to the bone. I sigh and follow the delicious smells down the hall to the top of the stairs. My mouth is watering, but I refuse to get my hopes up. Just because the woman can cook doesn't mean she's a nice person. Moriah Cade could cook if she wanted to.

I push my fears aside and slowly descend to the main floor. Taz Robbins doesn't survive by worrying; she survives by hiding behind a mask of attitude.

Kate is at the stove frying bacon. A boy about my age is sitting at the table, talking to her. They both look up as I come over.

Kate surprises me with a smile and a 'good morning', and the boy cocks his head at me. The light over the table glints off the strawberry highlights in his wavy blonde hair.

"You Taz?" he asks, studying me. I nod, a little uncomfortable under his scrutiny, and he holds out his hand.

"Chase. I'm your next-door neighbour," he says as he shakes my hand. It feels weird to be shaking hands with a kid my age, but if this is how they do it around here…hey, who am I to judge?

"I come over every Saturday morning to help muck out the

goat pens. In exchange, I get the best breakfast around," he continues, winking at Kate.

She waves a spatula at him. "I'm gonna tell your mom you said that," she threatens.

"Go ahead. She'll agree with me," Chase returns.

I stand there, shifting from foot to foot. Their easy banter makes me uncomfortable. In my world, adults and kids are worst enemies.

Kate brings several steaming platters over and sets them on the table. I warily slide into the chair across from Chase.

Kate sits at the head of the table and closes her eyes. I've been in a few religious homes, so I know what to do. Kate says a simple prayer, much different than the ones Mr. Ferguson used to say. He was a Methodist minister, and his prayers were like sermons, full of flowery descriptions of his children and wife, and pleas for mercy on my soul.

After the prayer, I dig in. Chase is right- this is the best breakfast ever, and I'm not going to let it go to waste. I listen to him and Kate discuss the goats, and soon realize they haven't mucked out the pens yet. Apparently, breakfast comes first. I'm hoping I don't have to help, which is unlikely. Slogging through goat poop is not my idea of a good time. But it soon becomes obvious that Kate is planning for me to meet her pets up close and personal today.

"Chase, show Taz the closet in the mudroom. There's an old pair of overalls in there that don't fit me anymore," Kate instructs as she clears the table. "I don't know what size boots you wear, but feel free to try on anything and everything in that room. I'm sure you'll find something."

The mudroom is a sunny room tucked away at the back of the house. It smells faintly like animal waste and sweat. Rows of muddy rubber boots line a mat by the back door, and the closet is overflowing with dirty coats, hats, overalls, and gloves.

"How does one lady use all this stuff?" I mutter as I follow Chase to the closet.

He laughs. "Kate keeps clothes here for all her nieces and nephews, too. Plus, she has her barn overalls, her gardening overalls, her yard work pants…you get the idea." He digs through the stinky mess in the closet and soon emerges with a pair of denim overalls. The straps are fraying, and colourful plaid patches grace the knees.

"I think these are the ones she meant. Try 'em on."

I wrinkle my nose at the smell as he hands them to me. I hold them up with two fingers.

"Have these things been washed recently?" I ask. There is no way I'm crawling into something that smells like it's straight from the manure factory, if there is such a thing.

Chase looks surprised. "I don't know. They haven't been worn recently, and they look clean to me. Why?"

"They smell," I retort, letting them drop from my fingers into a heap on the floor.

Chase throws back his head and laughs until his eyes are watering.

"Well, of course they stink. They're barn clothes. You don't think we wear our Gucci's in the goat pens, do you?"

I'm not that stupid. I doubt Chase even owns anything from Gucci. But either my memory has faded, or the farm I lived on when I was five didn't smell this bad. I don't appreciate Chase mocking me, though, so I hold my breath and pull the overalls up over my favourite pair of jeans. I grimace and fasten the straps over my shoulders.

"There. How's that, farmer boy?" I shoot back. Chase looks up from where he's already pulling on his boots and gives me a thumbs up.

"Now you need boots." He grins.

Kate comes in, and soon I'm outfitted in a pair of rubber

boots that clunk with each step. I follow Kate and Chase out to the barn, feeling like I've morphed into an elephant. The toe of my boot catches on the cracked cement step up to the barn, and I fall into Chase. He stumbles, and we both end up on the hay-strewn floor of the barn. The commotion sets off a chorus of bleating from the pens. I can feel my cheeks getting red as I scramble to my feet and give Chase a hand up. He's laughing at me again.

"Boots gettin' to ya?" he teases. I turn my back to him.

There are four pens in the barn, filled with chattering, multi-coloured fuzzballs. An adult goat, no bigger than a Border Collie, thrusts her nose out and bumps my hand.

"That's Dakota. She loves head scratches," Chase says, reaching out to give the brown and white goat a rub behind the ears. She's in the center pen with half a dozen other animals.

"Do they all have names?" I ask politely. They are kind of cute, but I really don't care for these smelly creatures. That is, I don't care until I see a tiny black kid in the pen across the aisle with its mama. The baby goat is the size of a small cat, and its mouth is curved in a permanent smile.

"Whoa!" I breathe, running over. I lean down over the pen and let the mama goat sniff my fingers. The kid comes up to investigate before dashing back behind its mama to safety. Another kid leaves its mother's side and sidles my way. I move my hand to scratch my other arm, and the sudden movement scares the little baby. It leaps back to safety.

"What's this one's name?" I ask Kate, pointing to the first kid. She grins from down the aisle, where she is pushing hay to a pen full of billy goats.

"That little guy doesn't have one yet. His mom's name is Sahara, and his dad is this big brown billy, Jasper. This is where the mamas and babies go until weaning age. The little ones are weaned in the far pen and stay there until they're sold."

Chase takes me on a tour of the rest of the small barn while Kate finishes pushing in the hay.

"That's the billy goat pen. The billies are the male goats," he informs me, as if I'm some city slicker.

"Let me guess- this pen is full of nannies. Those are the female goats," I jump in sarcastically, pointing to the pen where Dakota is now munching hay. Chase looks surprised.

"I'm not an idiot," I tell him. Even if I can barely walk in rubber boots and hate smelly overalls.

Chase shrugs. "Sorry. Didn't mean to offend you. Now, let's get mucking."

I follow him into a pen, feeling a little embarrassed for being so snarky. My attitude has always protected me before, but for some reason, I'm starting to care what this blonde, hick-town farmer boy thinks. I'll have to work on that.

Mucking turns out to be less horrible than I had imagined. My job is to help Chase move the goats to the outdoor yard and keep them from coming back inside, while Kate shovels out the dirty bedding with a small green tractor. It would actually be kind of fun, especially when we're letting out the baby pen, if it weren't for the smell. I'm starting to get dizzy from trying not to breath too deeply. I hope this is a once-a-year job.

I shut the last gate and bolt for the door. Chase follows me at a more leisurely pace, laughing, most likely at me. I sigh and gulp in a big breath of fresh air. There's till a tinge of goat in it, but it's better than in the barn.

Kate parks the tractor and comes over to us.

"Well, Taz, how was your first time in a goat barn?" she asks, eyes bright.

"People actually do this stuff for fun?" I choke out between great lungfuls of fresh air.

I expect a sharp retort, but she just laughs. "These are my money-makers. Most of those animals have awards and pedigrees.

I sell some of the better goats for breeding, others for pets, and keep the best ones for my herd. Petting zoos across the country come to me for goats. The offspring born here are known to be gentle and even-tempered."

Chase starts asking Kate about the goats, using lots of big words and important sounding things that make no sense to me. I head across the lawn to the back door. What I need right now is a shower.

I head upstairs to the massive bathroom that Kate said is all mine- her bedroom has an en suite, apparently- but stop halfway down the hall. The door to my left is open, and I can see a big computer screen in there. I jog to my room and look out the window. Kate and Chase are still deep in conversation, so I head back to the office. Leaving the door and my ears wide open, I open the screen with a click. Not surprisingly, I need a password to get in. But I've been in this situation many times before, so it doesn't take long to get around the security measures and into my email account.

I met AJ when I was eight. I'd escaped from my second foster home and was hiding out in an abandoned alleyway until the heat died down a bit. My first escape had only lasted ten hours, and I was determined to stay on the streets a little longer this time. AJ and a friend of his had found me, alone and cold, and taken me to their 'house', a cozy spot under a nearby bridge. Instead of taking advantage of me, AJ had taught me.

One of the first things he did was take me to a library in the next town over and helped me set up an email account. He had saved three contacts for me- his, his good friend Micah's, and one I was only to message in an absolute emergency. Most of the homes I've been in since have had a computer, and I've become very efficient at midnight tech runs and hacking the system. Over the years, I've exchanged a thousand messages with AJ, and a few with Micah when AJ was either 'unavailable' or in custody for a few nights. I've never had to contact the third person, and I hope I never will.

The house is still silent, so I open a new email and type a quick message to Micah. AJ had mentioned Micah was still in Des Moines, where we were going to head before we got caught, and I need to let him know what happened to us.

As I hit 'send', I hear a crash from above me. I jump out of the chair, and it rolls towards the wall. I grab the armrest a second before it would have hit the drywall and shove it up against the desk. I run from the office to my room and peer out the window. Chase and Kate are still talking outside. More thumping comes from above me, and I jerk around. What kind of rats live in this attic? I wasn't aware that there was a third story to this place.

The stink on my clothes is starting to get on my nerves, so I change as fast as I can, fingers fumbling with the buttons on my shirt. I opt out of a shower to go look for a hidden staircase instead and make my way slowly back to the base of the stairs. I examine the reading nook, the spare bedroom, and the linen closet, all with no results. There's nothing in my room, and the only unusual thing about Kate's room is the size of the bathtub in her en suite. You could raise baby hippos in that thing.

I'm about to give up when I discover it, way down at the end of the hallway. A pair of narrow steps is hidden behind a white door. I listen in the hallway for any sounds of Kate or Chase before tiptoeing up the stairway. Another white door is at the top, and I ease the knob a fraction of an inch to the right. It's locked.

I press my ear to the door. I can hear humming noises coming from beyond the wood. It definitely sounds like human humming, not rat humming. Does Kate have another foster child that she keeps locked up here? Will she lock me up here tomorrow, and let this person out for the day? Or maybe she hides criminals running from the police. This could be a great opportunity. Micah could help AJ break out, and I could hide him up here…

The sound of running water interrupts my wild fantasies, and footsteps walk right past the door, causing me to jerk back. My foot catches on the edge of the step below me, and I'm falling, arms whacking the walls on either side of the steps. I manage to catch onto the railing halfway down to the second floor. I lean against the wall, unhurt. But the element of surprise is gone. No doubt the person above now knows that someone was up here. I shakily descend the rest of the way and shut the door behind me. It's best to forget about everything I heard.

* * *

Chase and Kate talk most of the morning before he finally leaves. By the time Kate comes in and starts preparing lunch, I've snooped in pretty much every nook and cranny of the big house. The main floor has a massive rec room, with a closet full of toys and a flat screen TV the size of the dining room table. For a minute, I wonder who uses the toys, but then I remember Chase telling me about Kate's nieces and nephews. How many does she have, and how often do they visit? Do they live close by? How many new 'relatives' do I have? The questions race through my brain, but one thing is certain: when they come, they'll be the ones who take Kate's love. There is always some blood relative who takes up most of the attention, leaving us foster kids in the background. Sometimes the parents don't try to give them more attention; it just happens. Other times, they tell me to my face that I'm 'charity'; their good deed for the year so Santa brings them presents instead of coal.

Kate calls me to the table, and the meal is awkwardly silent without Chase there to chatter. Kate does drop one bombshell on me- I'm starting school on Monday. That's in two days.

As many times as I've been the 'new kid' at school, it never gets easier. I was always the one who never got invited anywhere, was never included, got bullied…you get the idea. When I was younger, I cared, but I've learned to stop doing that over the years. Caring has never helped me in any way. But not caring doesn't stop me from hating school.

Kate also offers to take me shopping that afternoon. I shrug. I know I could use more clothes, especially since my mostly black wardrobe will stick out in the crowds of blue jeans and cowboy boots, or whatever these country kids wear. But if she's only doing it to make herself look good, then I don't need her charity.

"It's your choice," she adds after a moment of silence. "I know at your age, I was a lot more into clothes than I am now, but maybe you aren't. It's just, with the farm and all, you'll need double the outfits."

I glance up from my plate of mac 'n' cheese. Like I'm planning to visit the barn everyday. Also, why is she being so nice? But I tell her I guess I could use a few things. I might as well stock up now, for the future. I'll need more clothes if I ever make it to Des Moines and start a real life on my own.

Kate glances at my bone-dry hair and adds, "You might want to shower before we go to town. Just saying."

There's nothing more humbling than a farmer saying I stink.

CHAPTER 3

Kate's brand-new Chevrolet pickup truck barely fits in the parking space at the local department store. Kate promises to take me to the mall next weekend if I don't find anything I like. I shrug; Walmart clothes are good enough.

There's no one else in the clothes department, so I take my time picking out a few half decent outfits. I know it doesn't matter if I show up to school on Monday in George or Louis Vuitton. Either way, I'm still the weird kid who should be locked up. I wonder if any of the other parents will let their kids hang out with me.

An old lady with prominent chin hair sidles up to us as we head for the checkout.

"Well, well, Kate Brighton, who do you have here?" she asks in the raspy voice common among the elderly. Her expression tells me she knows exactly who I am; she just wants to hear any extra details so she can pass them along at Tuesday Night Bingo.

Kate surprises me by putting an arm around my shoulders, as if shielding me from the old lady. "Hello, Mrs. Bennitt. This is my daughter, Taz."

Every muscle in my body screams as I fight the urge to jerk away in shock. No one has ever called me their daughter before. 'Foster daughter' maybe, or even 'state child'. One man, who was a fan of fantasy shows, used to call me his fosterling, but no one says I'm their daughter. I can't decide if I like it or not. I'm definitely not ready to call Kate my mom. With my record, I'll be somewhere else in a few months, anyway.

Mrs. Bennitt moves on, and Kate mutters an apology in my ear.

"Sorry, Taz. Welcome to a small town. Everyone's nosy."

"Then can I wait a few days to start school? Let things die down a little...?" I try.

Kate laughs. "Nice try, kiddo. I've got strict instructions to get your eyes in front of a white board. You've had haphazard schooling as it is."

Who told her that? Moriah couldn't care less if I missed a few days of school. In fact, my decent grades despite changing schools twice a year is a thorn in her flesh. She must have been a hard learner.

We grab a backpack and lunch pail, then head for the checkout. We make it through without getting sidetracked by any more grannies, and head for home.

As we pull into the driveway, I immediately notice something different. The gray Honda Civic that was sitting in the middle of the three-car garage when we left is gone. I had assumed it belonged to Kate, but maybe whoever was thumping away in the attic owns it. I almost ask Kate whose it is, but I chicken out at the last second. The day is going good so far, and I don't want to spoil the peace by getting an 'it's-none-of-your-business' lecture.

Kate heads out to feed the goats while I unpack my new clothes. Thankfully, she seems to agree that once in the barn is enough for me today. I stack the garments into the dresser in record time, then head for the computer. I'm dying to try the door to the attic again, in case the gray car was that person, and the attic is accessible now, but a response from Micah is more important. I'm doubtful he'll have responded already, but it's worth a look.

I log into my email. To my surprise, there's one new message, and I click it.

to: taz4ever
from: micdawson
subject: re: the bro

hey taz,
was wondering y u hadn't shown up yet. too bad
ab the bro. do u know where he is? know people
all over so maybe i can get a line in
hang in there,
M

Micah's spelling is atrocious, but the message is clear. Micah knows people in the right places, so he can get to AJ and communicate much better then anyone else I know.

I sit back in my chair, hesitating. Officer What's-His-Face made it clear that I'm expected to keep my nose clean from now on or else. I have my doubts that Kate will want me forever; nobody wants a fourteen-year-old kid with a record of running away. I still don't know why Kate even agreed to take me. But I've been here one day. I should give my final chance a bit longer of a chance before I throw it away. The minute someone finds this email, it's game over. I'm quite sure none of the ways Micah uses to establish off-the-record communication are legal. And as far as where AJ is…well, they didn't tell me. I'm the last person they'll tell.

A door creaks open downstairs, and I quickly exit out of the computer and tiptoe to my room.

Micah and AJ will have to wait.

CHAPTER 4

The rest of the weekend passes far faster than I would like. I take Sahara's little baby, whom Kate has named Cairo, out to play on the lawn Saturday evening. He, at least, doesn't smell like a mix of rotting eggs and moldy hay. Kate doesn't drag me to church on Sunday, because she says I 'need time to settle in before being dumped in a pew with Mrs. Bennitt and her friends'. I agree, although dumping me into a desk in front of twenty ninth graders on Monday is more unsettling. But Kate sticks to her guns and says, "I have strict instructions to get you in school ASAP." There are only two and a half months left. If it was up to me, I wouldn't finish out this year at all. And then there's the community service- ten hours a week after school and on Saturdays, serving meals and changing sheets at the old folk's home. In other words, it's ten hours a week in a sauna that smells weird.

I stand in front of my dresser Monday morning and try to decide which outfit will help me blend in the best. I'm good at blending in- that's why most of my clothes are shades of gray and black. Finally, I close my eyes and shove a hand into the drawer. A basic white tee and black jeans- perfect. I yank my hair back into a ponytail and head downstairs.

Kate is at the stove, frying up a meat, potato, and egg mixture that smells amazing. In the three days I've been here, I've learned that Kate is a regular country chef. I've gained three pounds so far. But I don't mind, because I'm skinnier than an ostrich's neck.

I squirm through Kate's prayer, especially the part where she prays that I will have a good day at school. If there is a God up there, I don't mind if you petition Him for me, but please don't do it when I'm within hearing distance.

After wolfing down my breakfast, I sit on the couch and restlessly tap my fingers together while Kate very slowly does the dishes and sweeps the floor. The minute hand on the antique clock hanging beside the fireplace inches to the next number, and Kate puts the broom away and motions me toward the door. I jump up and rush out the truck.

The air rushes in and out of my lungs in short bursts as the vehicle rolls into town. I clutch one of my backpack straps until my fingers go numb. Thankfully, Kate doesn't say anything. I don't need her to mother me.

Oakville High School is a sprawling red brick building on the east side of town, within walking distance of Main Street. The parking lot is full when we get there, even though it's still ten minutes before the bell will ring.

Kate leads me up the front steps. I feel like I'm running the gauntlet as kids turn to gawk at us. Hi, I'm Taz. I'm the criminal who's staying with the lovely Miss Brighton. No, I will not poison her or steal her grandmother's diamond brooch.

I bite back a smile. Maybe, if my homeroom teacher makes me introduce myself in front of the class, I'll say that. They're all thinking it, anyway.

I hunch my shoulders as we enter the packed hallway and wish I hadn't pulled my hair back. I've used my dark locks as a curtain for my face more times than I can count. Kate breaks a path through the students ahead of me, and I try to stay as close as possible without stomping on her heels. It seems like hours later when we finally reach the main office.

The woman behind the front desk is pleasantly plump, with curly brown hair tied in a knot on top of her head. She's sitting in a baby blue chair, typing with one hand while the other one writes madly in a planner. A half empty box from Krispy Kreme balances precariously on top of a stack of student records. She smiles at us as we enter.

"Hello, you must be Taz!" She grins, pausing her multi-tasking and setting down her pen. "It's so good to have you here!"

I've been to a few of these small-town schools over the years, and they are the worst. It's much harder to hide in a crowd of a hundred than in a crowd of six hundred. The secretary will probably page the whole school to introduce the new kid.

"Hi, Lauren. I'm here to get a schedule for Taz set up. All the other paperwork has been filled out for her," Kate says briskly.

Man, she's efficient, I mutter to myself. I've been here three days, and it's not like Kate knew ahead of time I was coming. And yet somehow, she has everything set up.

Lauren lifts herself from the chair with a sigh and sashays over to a dented mental filing cabinet in the corner. She emerges a few moments later with a stack of papers.

"Yes, yes. I have them here," she says with another grin, plopping back in her chair. Her elbow nudges the box of donuts, and they wobble dangerously. She doesn't seem to notice.

She shuffles through the forms before looking up at me.

"I see here you were enrolled in a history class, a math class, and a science class at your previous school. Those are the important ones. You also had…let me see…art, study hall, and…" she stops and squints at the paper, "Irish dancing!"

I bite back a giggle. Art and Irish dancing were fillers- easy electives I rarely attended, anyway.

"I'm sorry, but we don't have Irish dancing here at Oakville. You will have to choose something else. Perhaps theater would interest you?" Lauren pulls a laminated sheet out of the mess of papers on her desk and hands it to me. It's a list of electives I can take, and I scan through it, looking for an easy one.

"Uh…I'll take Foods Class," I decide. That could be fun.

Maybe I could even learn how to cook as well as Kate. Or I'll skip it every day and eat a snack for my 'Foods Class'.

"Wonderful!" Lauren beams. "What an excellent choice! Foods is one of my favourite classes, especially when they bring me the leftovers."

The bell chimes loudly, and Lauren leaps out of her chair, sending it flying into the wall behind her. She places her hand over her heart and hisses, "Stand up straight! The national anthem is coming on!"

After the anthem, like a typical small-town school, we also have to endure the Lord's Prayer. Actually, I seemed to be the only one enduring it. Lauren clenches her eyes shut so tight her cheeks and eyebrows meet each other, and Kate folds her hands respectfully and smiles through the prayer. I stand there and absentmindedly survey the corny posters on the walls. I'm not sure how I feel about the whole God thing.

Kate leaves after that to do some work- she works from home, doing money things for a company based out of Des Moines- and Lauren leads me to my homeroom class. I love having math class first thing in the morning when I'm still half asleep.

The class is at the far end of the building, so poor Lauren is puffing like a draft horse by the time we get there. She doesn't quite have the strength to knock on the door, so I do it while she leans heavily against the wall.

"Mr. Avery…huff puff…this is…Taz. Taz…huff puff…meet Mr. Avery," she stammers as soon as the door opens. "Bye Taz…I need to go get…my inhaler."

With that, she turns on her heel and heads back to her desk, leaving me standing awkwardly in the doorway in front of fifteen smiling students. Barf.

Mr. Avery directs me to an empty seat in the back row, beside a girl with shockingly orange curls. A host of freckles dance across her face, and her green eyes sparkle at me as I sit down.

She leans across the aisle.

"Hey! I'm Chloe!" she whispers. "What's your name?"

I'm sure she already knows my name, but I love that she lets me introduce myself. Mr. Avery goes back to teaching as though a new kid didn't just walk in, so Chloe keeps chattering to me.

"I live on a farm on the other side of the Colbys. Have you met Chase Colby yet? He's super nice. You live on the other side of him, right?"

I nod, and she keeps on whispering, "What classes do you all have? I have history next. We'll have to compare classes."

"I have history next, too." I whisper back. At least I'll walk into that class knowing *one* name. And Chloe seems okay; a little bit of a pushover, maybe, but what else can you expect from a small-town girl who's never been farther than Kalona?

"Chloe Davidson. Can you tell me what kind of angle this is?" Mr. Avery interrupts us. He gives Chloe a stern look over his wire-rimmed glasses.

"Uh…obtuse!" Chloe replies after a second.

"Correct. However, I would appreciate if you kept your eyes on the board, even if you think you have angles all figured out."

Instead of being embarrassed, Chloe gives him a charming grin and folds her hands on her lap.

Mr. Avery actually rolls his eyes at her before turning back to the board. The math teacher I had in Ottumwa would have completely embarrassed you, made you answer every single question for the rest of the lecture, and given you a detention for whispering. These small-town teachers are something else.

I sneak a sideways look at Chloe. She sees me looking and points her nose to the board, giving me a mock glare. I press my lips together to hold back my laughter.

Soon, Mr. Avery hands out a worksheet full of triangles. He stops at my desk as he places on on my desk and crouches down to my level.

"Let me know how this compares to your other school," he whispers. "If its stuff you haven't learned yet, I'll make sure to get you caught up."

I nod and wish he'd move on. I don't need a teacher crouching beside me, staring into my face. I don't bother telling him that I learned about this stuff a month ago. He'll figure it out.

I whip through the math paper and finish the class by doodling in the margins with a red pen, so it looks like I'm busy. As I follow Chloe out the door, I quickly slip my page into Mr. Avery's 'to be marked' bin. He doesn't see me.

I hide behind Chloe in history, awkwardly being the 'teacher's helper' for an experiment in science and sit alone at lunch in the cafeteria. At least, that's what I do until Chloe finds me again. She introduces me to a bunch of people. The only face I remember doesn't belong to any of her friends, though. It belongs to a dark-haired girl sitting in a corner all by herself, her face carefully blank of all expression. I meet her gaze, chin up, and the mask slips for a moment, revealing suspicion mixed with open curiosity. Then her expression returns to nothing, and we both go back to our lunch. But that glimpse of honesty behind her tough façade pulls at me, and I think about her for the rest of lunch.

In my next class, Foods, we watch a video on where lemons grow. It's the perfect soundtrack for a nap, but unfortunately the extra sleep doesn't give me the energy boost I crave. After a tough experiment in science, I'm ready to crash. Luckily, the only class I have left is Art. I debate skipping, but figure that's kind of a dumb thing to do on my first day. I have a feeling Kate would give me more goat chores if I did that. Oh, well- hopefully I can snag a chair in the back and sleep this one out, too.

I walk into Art 101 three minutes after the bell. The studio is tucked away down a short hallway by the furnace room, and it takes me forever to find it. Students are busy shuffling through things and getting supplies, filling the room with a dull roar.

A small, elderly woman looks up from the front and smiles as I enter. Her gray hair is swept up in a knot, with at least four pencils and a paintbrush protruding from the mound. I muster a smile and search for an empty seat in the back corner.

"Hello, Taz," she says. Her voice isn't loud, but solid and firm, and it reaches every corner of the room. A few kids look up. Most of them smile at me before returning to their work.

The teacher, Mrs. Woodrow, according to my schedule, motions me up to her desk. I reluctantly comply.

"I see you did art at your previous school. I don't know what you have all studied, as art curriculums can vary widely from place to place. However, my class is more about expressing your creativity than it is about becoming the next Picasso. I am a strong believer in 'unimaginative art is dead art'. We do look at some techniques, of course, but I, or another student, can help you with those as the need arises. I'm sure you will do fine in here," she reassures me.

I nod and smile on the outside while grimacing on the inside. I always did despise the teachers who were all about 'reaching your best potential'. The ones who don't care let you catch a nap, and rarely worry if you don't pull your weight. But teachers like Mrs. Woodrow are always on your tail if you slack.

"We are finishing a project that will be due by Friday, and its a bit of a longer one, so I won't make you start on that," Mrs. Woodrow goes on. "You are welcome to explore the classroom, look at other projects, or experiment with any medium you want. Oh, and your seat is midway back in the row along the wall, beside Ivan." She points to an empty chair beside a tall, dark-haired boy with a crew cut.

Oh, brother. Assigned seats, I moan to myself as I head over.

Someone catches my eye as I slip into the green metal chair. It's Chase, waving at me from the back row. And his seatmate is the girl with black hair from the cafeteria.

CHAPTER 5

"Make sure to give the pregnant nannies that extra supplement," Kate reminds me, throwing a forkful of hay to the billy goats.

I grimace and scoop out some dusty-smelling pellets from the blue bin. I've been here almost three weeks, and I've learned more than I ever wanted to about goats. Unfortunately, Kate thinks there's a lot more I need to know. She's decided to make me come out to the barn one morning a week. I get to pick which morning, but still. She says 'a few chores never hurt anyone' but I beg to differ. My head hurts from the high-pitched bleating, and my back aches from forking hay.

After a shower and breakfast, I sit outside on the porch to wait for Kate. The weather is getting warmer, and despite a brisk wind, I'd rather be out here with the birds than inside watching Kate do dishes. Inside there is always the danger she will ask me to help. I close my eyes and let the sunshine wash over me.

So far, this place isn't so bad. As much as I complain about the barn chores, they're nothing compared to what I've dealt with at previous places. Kate is nice enough, and I get lots of free time to explore or do homework. I always struggled to get my homework done at the Baker's. Taking care of her five brats while she read her favourite novel took a lot out of me. I'm a little on edge, waiting for the ax to fall. Most places I've stayed at eventually take a turn for the worst.

Tires crunching on gravel jerks me back to full consciousness.

A dark gray Honda Civic is crawling up the lane at a snail's pace. I stand up and stare as the car boldly drives up to the garage. It's the same car that was parked beside Kate's pickup truck a few weeks ago. I haven't seen it or heard the mysterious noises from the attic, which I'm pretty sure are related, since then.

The Civic creeps to a stop inches from the garage door. The windows have zero tint, so I stare at the driver. Most of her face is hidden in the shadow of a dark blue beret. She looks like an artist.

Kate comes running out of the house with my backpack on her arm.

"C'mon, Taz, we're gonna be late!" she pants, then skids to a stop beside me as the lady climbs out of her car.

"Oh, hi, Madame. I'm so sorry, I forgot you were coming today. Feel free to let yourself in and go up to your studio."

Madame whoever-she-is, is a short, stout woman in a woolen dress that matches her beret. Shoulder-length curls spill out from beneath her hat and sway like the bells of a wind chime as she nods. When she speaks, her voice is rich and melodious. Maybe she isn't an artist; she sounds like a music teacher.

Madame thanks Kate and disappears through the side door into the garage. I follow Kate to the truck, bursting with questions.

"Who is that?" I ask as soon as the truck door closes.

"Oh, that's Madame Lemair. She rents the attic space for her studio. She's a well-known painter actually and does paint therapy for children with autism and ADHD and such like."

Well. I guess now I know who haunts the attic.

"Chase's younger brother comes quite often," Kate adds. "He hasn't been feeling well the past few weeks, but I'm guessing you'll see him around soon. Parker's the sweetest kid, and painting has helped him a lot."

Chase has siblings? A brother? An odd feeling rises in my

chest, spinning around like a funnel cloud. If he's ashamed of them, I'd like to realign some things in his brain, or at least on his face. I know I don't have much to say, considering the number of siblings I have, exactly zero last time I checked, but shunning someone of your own blood is wrong. You might not like them all the time, but they're family.

"Parker has autism," Kate explains. "His family is so glad to see him enjoy something like painting so much; it's bringing him out of his shell. Chase, especially, has been relieved. He worries too much about his siblings."

Okay, my assumptions were way off. I think my brain is the one that needs some realignment.

Maybe Chase didn't tell me about his brother to protect Parker. Maybe Chase doesn't trust me. The thought makes me uncomfortable, so I push it away. Who cares what Chase or anybody else thinks about me? And it's not like I trust him.

Kate pulls up in front of the school, and I hop out. I slam a mental door on my thoughts as the truck door closes behind me.

Chloe is sick today, so I have no one to tag after. I whip through my math paper and leave Mr. Avery wondering what to do with me. I ignore him and pretend to sleep. The rest of the morning goes okay. I'm starting to put a few more names and faces together, so classes are a little less awkward.

I sit by myself in a corner at lunch. I feel weird sitting with Chloe's friends when she's not here, because I don't know them that well. Plus, none of them are as cool as Chloe. Shelby giggles too much, Piper rolls her eyes at everything, and Sienna thinks she's funny when she's really not. The three of them can get super annoying without Chloe there to balance them out.

Someone slides their tray into my field of vision, and I look up, expecting it to be Chase taking pity on me. Instead, it's his seatmate- in Art, at least. The girl sinks down in the chair across from me. I keep chewing as though she's nothing special, and we size each other up in silence. Finally, she nods once and says, "Name's Talia. Talia Hayes."

I pause long enough to let her know I'm not one of those kids who's desperate to make new acquaintances. The silences and expressions and words are all part of some odd, unexplainable game I learned to play well out on the streets. You have to act disinterested, but not too much, or you'll lose out on a possibly beneficial connection.

"Taz," I say finally, before turning back to my cafeteria pasta and chicken.

"So, you've been here awhile?" she asks after a bit.

I look up again. "About three weeks. You?"

"All my life," she says. "And most days, it's the most boring place on earth."

"Yup. Guess what my…guardian…calls fun? Goats," I reply sarcastically. "Got a whole herd of them."

Talia cracks a smile. "Pretty much all that the people around here are into is animals. Your neighbour boy, there- his family has a whole herd of cows, around forty or so, and some chickens and pigs to boot."

"Who, Chase?"

She nods.

"Well, that must not be enough for him, because he likes to come muck out goats, too," I add. She barks out a harsh laugh.

I wasn't planning to throw dirt on Chase, but I've finally met someone who fits my old life, and although I'd never admit it, I could use a person like Talia in my life- someone unpredictable, yet safe; someone who will leave you hanging unless you're 'in' with them, then they'll die for you; someone who won't ask for secrets but will bring you along for the ride.

We eat in silence for awhile, each trying to choke down what the school considers 'food'. Finally, Talia looks up again.

"If you're ever looking for a bit of excitement," she says

casually, "Head up to the old brick factory on the hill. It's hidden in the woods, and people like to do a bit of bike racing on the weekends, if you know what I mean. Nothing fancy- the track's only a timed single, but it works."

I do know what she means. Back when I was eleven or so, I stayed in a high-rise apartment in Los Angeles. There was an old track a few blocks from the building, close enough to hear the bass thumping, and it was always hopping anytime past midnight. From my bedroom window on the twenty-ninth floor, I could watch the races, often staying up past my bedtime for the show. I'd collect random trinkets from around the room and bet, with a bunch of stuffed animals as my opponents. More often than not, I'd end up with nothing. Sometimes the police would show up to try to bust the gambling rings, and the park would erupt into a riot of sirens and squealing tires. Those were the most interesting nights. And dirt bikes can make just as good entertainment as cars.

"Where is this place?" I ask, careful to conceal my eagerness. Talia gives me a knowing look. She knows I'm in, and for a bit I'm afraid she'll try to get something out of it for herself- make me pay for the address or something. But she smiles and finally answers with, "Meet me Saturday night, no later then 11:45, at the far corner of the soccer field behind the school. I'll show you the way."

Doing this will break the agreement I signed back in Ottumwa. But what's life if you can't live on the edge once in awhile? Taz Robbins is certainly no rule-follower, and AJ would be proud of me. Secrets divide, and I need to watch how close I get to Kate. She's nice enough to trust, which is dangerous for an orphan like me.

I can't wait for Saturday.

* * *

There's a sliver of moon in the sky, giving me a lopsided sneer as I jump out from beneath the covers, fully dressed. Tonight couldn't come fast enough, after a day at the retirement home cleaning up messes and folding linens. The door creaks a little as I slip out into the hall, and I hold my breath as I pass the door to Kate's bedroom. All is silent.

I slip into my new black Nike's- I wrecked my other ones in the goat pen yesterday after forgetting to change into boots for morning chores- and leave the mansion behind.

I found an old blue bicycle in the garden shed yesterday, and Kate patched and blew up the tires for me. I took a run around the property with it, to make Kate think that biking is my new favourite pastime, and it runs all right. The steering is a little messed up, and the seat it too low, but it'll get me to town and back.

I don't think about what will happen if Kate wakes up and finds me missing. I'm not supposed to go off the property alone. Instead, I think about AJ winking at me from inside a correctional facility as I ease around the rules. I stay as far over on the road as possible, ready to hit the ditch at any moment. An owl hoots somewhere in the distance, sending shivers down my spine. Owls sound so lonesome and ghostly.

I crest a small hill and see a pair of headlights off in the distance. I steer in behind a tree and wait for the vehicle to pass. It's an old Ford truck with a small livestock trailer behind it. The trailer sounds like a train wreck, and one wheel wobbles dangerously. That's all I see before it's gone over the hill. I wonder if it's a criminal, hauling stolen goods around. After all, who else would be out in the middle of the night in these parts?

I reach the edge of town and take the back streets to the school. The town is ominously quiet- I don't see a single soul out and about.

The grass is damp with dew as I make my way across the

soccer field. My shoes are squishy by the time I get to the back fence. A shadow steps from behind a tree, and Talia mumbles a greeting.

"Dump the bike and follow me," she says, before darting across the lawn. I hurry after her. In this situation, Talia is in control.

I observe my surroundings as we head past the schoolyard and across an empty lot. Talia might be in the lead this time, but I can get here myself from now on.

The streetlights soon fade into shadows, and the terrain slopes upward as we make our way through the forest surrounding Oakville. Spongy earth turns to gravel as we hit a long, winding road up into the hills. I'm out of breath by the time we burst free of the tree line and head across the old parking lot of the hulking, red factory. A dull roar floats from beyond the gloomy building.

"This is the brick factory. It makes bricks, and it's made of bricks," Talia comments as we go around the building.

"Whatever," I respond, biting back a grin. Was that supposed to be funny?

The roaring engines and pounding bass and smell of burning gasoline get stronger as we emerge into the back clearing.

There's a large hole behind the building, where the brick factory dug out clay, and hundreds of tires have since crisscrossed it into the trails and jumps and bridges of a bike racing track. The only lights are a few, small, battery-operated ones, and the headlights of a strategically placed truck at the end of a long driveway that slopes down into the pit. Talia was right- the track is only big enough to accommodate one bike at a time. It's not a 'real' race, with the vehicles sliding neck-and-neck around curves. Instead, the bikers compete for the fastest time, like a barrel race. Several people cluster in a large group on the rim, drinking and bellowing insults to each other. Talia pulls me away from them and leads me to a shadowy clump of trees.

"Those are all college kids and older high schoolers. They don't like us 'little babies' hanging around, but they'll tolerate us as long as we stay out of sight and keep quiet," my companion explains.

I nod. I can't see quite as good over here, but I've had enough run-ins with college kids to know that Talia's being smart. I still have a scar from when a college freshman busted me across the elbow with a broken bottle, after AJ and I snuck into a frat party for the food. (We were desperate.)

Down below us, a group of guys on dirt bikes are idling, talking big about their bikes and their abilities. One of them is shot gunning beers as fast as he can grab them, and I have my doubts he'll run the course straight.

An older guy, who must be out of college by now unless he's going for vet or brain surgeon, drives up to the edge of the pit in a metallic blue Camaro. The air tenses a little as he gets out, black leather briefcase in hand. He runs his index finger over his mustache and grooms his goatee while surveying the crowd. Satisfied with what he sees, he gives a slight nod and goes around to his trunk.

"That's the dealer," Talia whispers.

"I know. I'm not stupid!" I snarl back. There will never be an unregulated race without a shark or two to handle bets and fleece people cold.

"That's the worst of them all," Talia adds under her breath. I study the tall, thin man as he sets up shop. He's dressed in a black vest and a white shirt with frills around the sleeves. His thin mustache curls up at the ends, giving him a shrewd look. Definitely not an honest man.

Someone turns down the music, and a tall, sturdy blonde guy steps into the bed of the truck down in the pit. He grabs a mic and yells, "This is your host, Sandy. Now who's ready to partyyyyy???!!"

A chorus of eager shouts is his answer, and he goes on to introduce each of the drivers and the spots they have drawn. All the drivers have big show names, and even bigger egos. The driver who completes the course the fastest wins $300, and everyone is sure it'll be himself.

A big, burly, lumberjack type with a sleeveless black vest and a red bandana draws the first spot. Dirt spurts out from behind his rear tire as he pulls up to the tiny red flag that marks the beginning of the course. He flexes one bulging bicep at the crowd, making the coiled snake on his upper arm dance around. He angles his bike, so his front tire is a little over the line. It's easy to see from up here, but nobody else seems to notice.

"That there's Frog. Nobody knows his real name, or where he lives, but he shows up every Friday night. He's the best cheater of the whole bunch. He's nicknamed 'Frog' because his eyes bulge out, and his bike is green," Talia whispers in my ear. Money is rapidly exchanging hands as the bike takes off down the track. Frog screams around the first corner, the one side of his bike scraping the ground. He hits the first triple jump at breakneck speed and almost flips when his front wheel hits the dirt. He manages to right himself before looping through a large clay pipe and jumping a stack of logs. He sails over a small ditch and does a model flight over a corner jump. He speeds up over a straight stretch and has enough momentum to fly over the speed bumps beyond but misses the drop off right after. He plows through a large, shallow puddle near the top of the hill, wasting precious seconds. Up on the rim, a guy in a red shirt curses and throws his beer on the ground in frustration, watching his money disappear with Frog's costly mistakes.

Frog, annoyed that he missed the turn and ready to redeem himself, takes the dragon's back way too fast, and lands in the center of the rollers. My neck hurts for him as he jounces over the bumps to the finish line.

"Four minutes and forty-three seconds!" Sandy yells. The guy in the red shirt throws another beer can onto the ground and stomps on it. The shark smiles from beside his car.

"That's a slow ride for this tiny track," Talia murmurs in my ear. "The record time is 3:59:5,which is insane, and the average is around 4:35."

Frog takes his helmet off and throws it on the ground. He turns his back to the crowd and walks his bike up the driveway and out of sight.

The next rider is a guy dressed in a black jacket with a yellow tutu around his waist named Smiley. He takes the jumps slower, but he gets the drop off and all the corners and sails over the rollers, ending with a time three seconds better than Frog. The guy in the red shirt is tearing his hair out as he watches all his money disappear into the shark's shiny black briefcase.

The next few riders smash Smiley's time to pieces. Before long, a beefy woman with frizzy purple hair and her almost identical twin, except he's male and has orange locks, are tie for first place. The shark looks as satisfied as a cat with a bowl of cream as he collects heavy bets on who will win.

It looks like it's going to be a rematch when a small black bike comes rolling down the far side of the pit. The rider is clad in a black jacket with pink details, and the slight build suggests that it's a young female. A long, dark ponytail with hot pink tips streams out behind her helmet as she pulls up to the starting line.

"She came," Talia whispers in my ear.

"Who is she?" I whisper back, but Talia shushes me.

The crowd up on the rim behind the factory quiets down to a nervous hum. From the truck bed, Sandy shrugs helplessly down at the crowd of bikers circled near him. One of them gives him a slow nod, and he holds his stopwatch into the air. He doesn't countdown like he did for the rest of the bikers; he just yells 'Go'. I get the feeling this woman isn't exactly wanted on the track. But she's ready, and her bike leaps ahead at Sandy's word.

What happens next is magic. I've heard of animals and their riders being 'like one', but I've never seen it happen between a human and a machine before. But there's no other way to describe it. Her lithe body turns the corners with the bike, and when she lands after the jumps, she doesn't bounce in her seat at all. She jumps over the clay pipe instead of going through it, saving her precious seconds. She manages to clear the logs before leaping the ditch and executes an impossibly tight corner jump. She sails down the drop off and scales the dragon's back and the rollers before cruising over the finish line. She slows down in a wide arc before coming to a stop at the back bumper of the truck. The air is deathly still.

"Uh…four-sixteen point three," Sandy stutters into the mic.

The crowd erupts into a loud roar. Down below, the other riders look mad, especially the two people who were tie for first. They've been stood up by a smaller bike, with a tiny, child-like driver, no less.

Talia tugs my sleeve. The crowd is reaching a boiling point, and the bikers down below look ready to gang up and fight the girl with the pink tips.

"Let's go," Talia urges, pulling me to my feet.

I glance over my shoulder as the girl rider snatches the prize money from Sandy's hands and roars off into the night.

"Watch where you're going!" Talia hisses, jerking me away from a fallen log in my path. I turn back and follow her around the brick walls of the factory.

"Who is that?" I ask as soon as we're far enough down the driveway that no one can hear us.

Talia shrugs. "Nobody knows. She showed up a few times last summer, and once before this spring. She always wears that helmet with the tinted visor and shows up near the end of the race. Every time she's come, she's placed, and she always grabs the money and escapes before anyone can start a fight. Some people think the sharks are putting her up to it so they can get more money, but she's come at random enough times that it isn't likely. I know for a fact she came to a race where Owen Bradley was collecting bets, and he hates the guy who was here tonight, so I doubt they were working together. But she's an insane rider. The fastest time she's had was 4:09:3, and it was the season record last summer." Talia pauses to haul in a deep breath. Neither of us would admit it, of course, but I can tell that Talia is as fascinated as I am with the girl.

By the time I reach my bike, I've made up my mind to study every single person I come across for pink-tipped hair. The mystery rider has to live somewhere, after all. And Oakville isn't that big.

CHAPTER 6

The wind whips my hair around and makes my eyes water as I sail over the side of the pit. I've watched from the shadows, and 4:18:9 is the time to beat. Frog is in the lead currently, and the red shirt guy is finally happy he might win a little something tonight. Too bad for him- I'm here.

My bike rumbles beneath me, but the vibrations are just another part of my body. I don't even notice the shaking. I pull my gloves on and zip up the blue zipper on my jacket before pulling my tinted visor down over my face.

My nickname is 'Blue Mystery', and only Talia knows who I am. I've been trained by the Girl with the Pink Tips, who swore me to secrecy concerning her identity. She can no longer race, due to a hip injury, so I am taking her place. The race money is how she- and now me- supports herself, so I must win. I'm not worried, however, because my bike and I are one.

I choose this moment to roll down over the edge of the pit. Sandy scowls at me from the truck bed. Frog glowers from the shadows. The noise from up on the rim dies down. 'Blue Mystery' is here.

Sandy doesn't count down, but I'm ready for him. At the word 'go', I'm off, soaring over the triple jump like an eagle. Dirt flies up at my face, but my visor protects me from the elements. My stomach flips as I take a corner jump, and somersaults as I sail down the drop off. I know this race is shaping up to be one of my best.

A loud noise reaches through the helmet and bangs against my eardrums.

Thump-thump. Thump-thump-thump.

It's Frog, with a jackhammer, banging a large rock near the finish line. He's trying to distract me!

Thump-thump. It's working. Shut up, Frog!

The noise gets louder, jarring me out of a sound sleep. Kate is hammering on my bedroom door.

"Taz! Wake up!" she yells, and from the tone of her voice, I have a feeling it's not the first time. She jiggles the doorknob. Right. I locked it after coming home last nigh—er, this morning.

I groan and pull the covers over my head. It's the weekend, for crying out loud. Let me sleep in!

"Taz! You'd better get up and unlock the door before I call you by your real name!"

Okay, so she's mad. I've never heard Kate threaten me before. And what she just said is a valid threat.

"I'm coming!" I mumble, stumbling to the door with my eyes still closed. I clumsily unlock it and let her in.

"What time is it?" I growl.

"It's time for church," Kate announces, suddenly cheerful again. "I let you sleep through breakfast, but if you hurry, you might have time to grab a muffin on your way out."

My stomach stages a revolt at the mention of food, and I quickly decline.

Kate gives me a long once-over and shrugs. "Whatever you say. It's a long time until lunch. Now, you've got twenty minutes to make yourself look presentable."

A long time until lunch? What time is it, anyway? If it's not at least eleven o'clock, I have some words for her. I rub my bleary eyes and squint at my alarm clock.

"It's only nine-thirty!" I shriek at Kate's receding back. "Why in the world are you getting me up so early?" I haven't been to Kate's church yet. The first few Sundays, she listened at home while I daydreamed and pretended to pay attention. And last

Sunday, one of her goat mamas was kidding with twins, and she wanted to be home in case there were any complications. (There weren't.)

She swivels around at the top of the stairs. "I told you. We're going to church. And 9:30 is a completely reasonable time to get up, young lady. Especially since you got to bed early last night."

The way she says the last part makes me wonder if she suspects something's up, like maybe her foster kid wasn't at home last night. I clamp my mouth shut and keep the rest of my thoughts to myself. I don't need any questions from her.

"Now you've only got fifteen minutes left. So, hop to it," she says over her shoulder before disappearing down the steps.

I wonder what she would do if I wasn't ready in fifteen minutes, but then I have visions of Kate marching me to the front bench in my faded, Mickey Mouse pajamas I refuse to get rid of because they were the first gift I ever received, and decide I'd better not push my luck.

But Taz Robbins also wouldn't be caught dead in a pink, flowery dress with big sleeves and lace around the bottom, like the one that's been hanging neglected at the back of my closet since I got here. I do have a black skirt, though…a miniskirt. This town is full of staunch, modest Baptists, and I'm guessing at least some of them go to Kate's church, so this might be fun. I pair it with a red-checkered shirt and my white Vans for good measure and run a brush through my hair before hopping down the stairs.

Kate looks up from a thick book laid open on the kitchen table and surveys my outfit. Her mouth opens, and I stare back, daring her to say something. We fight a silent battle for a few seconds before she looks away, slams her book shut, and tucks it under one arm.

"Alright, then. Let's go."

The ride to church is quiet and the tension between us is as thick as a dictionary. I refuse to talk to Kate, and she refuses to look at me. I giggle in my head the whole way, thinking about what Mrs. Bennitt will say when she sees my outfit.

Kate pulls into the parking lot much too fast and has to slam on the brakes to avoid rear ending a minivan discharging kids by the bucketful. They're all dressed in little blue vests with deep red bow ties or frilly spring dresses in lavender and rose.

"What a nice family," I mutter sarcastically as Mom herds five kids through the front doors while Dad goes to park the van. Kate says nothing as she rolls into a parking spot near the graveyard out back.

She pulls the key from the ignition and sits there for a minute, looking at me. She opens and closes her mouth a few times, before finally turning away and getting out. I feel like a mischievous kid who avoided a lengthy lecture on proper behaviour.

I follow Kate across the parking lot. Inside the big, wooden front doors, a tall guy with floppy blonde hair and a navy suit pumps my hand until my arm is on fire.

"You must be Taz. Welcome. I'm Davis, the youth pastor here. We're so excited to have you join us!"

I'll admit I thought he was kind of cute until I heard the word 'pastor'. Davis looks like he belongs on a Baja beach with a surfboard, not in a church basement leading Bible study.

Kate heads for a pew near the middle, and I slide in after her. The pews are cushioned, and the dark blue fabric is surprisingly soft. Maybe church won't be so bad; I might even manage to fall asleep.

Someone across the aisle catches my eye. Chase is grinning and waving his fingers at me, trying to get my attention. He's all dressed up, in a button-down shirt and navy pants, but doesn't seem fazed by my choice of clothing. A small, dark-haired boy with big brown eyes is sitting beside him, and a curly blonde head is leaning against his mom's shoulder. They look like the perfect family. An unfamiliar feeling of longing shoots through me, catching me off guard as I watch them. His mom leans over and whispers something to his dad, and they both chuckle softly. They're even holding hands, and they've got to be, like, forty. I wonder if she's still his first wife. She certainly looks like she could be the mother of Chase and his siblings. Most people that old are divorced and crabby, not still in love with each other and their kids.

Chase and his little sister have caught me staring by now, so I turn toward the front. A tall man in a deep brown suit steps up to the pulpit. His thin frame looks like it belongs in a fence row, holding up a strand of barbed wire and a bird or two. He sets his large, black Bible on the pulpit with a thump and clears his throat with a low growl.

"Welcome, friends in Christ. I'm Pastor Chris…"

I amuse myself by counting all the shades of colour I can find in the sunshine streaming through the stained-glass windows. Everyone else seems to be enjoying whatever is coming out of the preacher's mouth. I soon lapse into a daydream about finding the Girl with the Pink Tips.

Around the half hour mark, I come back to earth, stifle a yawn, and shift in the pew. My tailbone is starting to ache, and my legs feel stiff. Kate looks up from where she is jotting notes in the margin of her Bible and gives me an understanding smile. Although I don't know how she could ever understand how long this feels to a kid like me. She grew up in church, after all.

Something she's written down catches my eye. God loves me.

It's highlighted in bright orange, and I wonder how three simple words could be so important to a person. And does God really love everyone? Does He love me?

I turn back to the windows. There's no point in asking. A street kid like me would never understand this God stuff. But at least I know there are forty-five shades of colour in the stained-glass windows.

CHAPTER 7

Dear Taz,

How are things in Oakville? I hope the food is better than what we get here. And more colourful. I'm getting tired of seeing gray. It's everywhere- gray walls, gray door, gray bars, gray floor… even the food is different shades of gray. At least our uniforms are coloured- they're bright red.

This place is okay, though. The guards could be worse, and I've made one kind-of friend. His name is Ash. He's cool. There are a lot of disagreements here, and its nice to have someone on your side.

If you're ever back in Ottumwa for some reason, and happen to see Jack, let me know, okay? I think about him some these days.

Okay, I gotta go now.

AJ

I fold the letter up with trembling hands.

'Stop it, Taz!" I berate myself. "It's just a letter!"

But I can read between the lines and see all the things AJ can't say because they would get censored out. Juvie sucks, the food sucks, the fighting sucks, and while the guards aren't vicious, they don't care, either.

AJ is a smooth talker. He doesn't pick fights if he can help it. AJ rolls over people with his words, not with his fists. By the looks of his letter, though, he's been at the receiving end of more than one 'disagreement'.

I wonder how he's doing. Is his face all scratched? Is his nose bashed in? Can he still see out of both eyes? Will he come out scarred and hardened, or even worse, broken beyond repair?

"It's juvie, Taz, not the zoo! They wouldn't let that happen!" I try to stop my steadily darkening thoughts. But I've heard stories of 'kid jail'- exaggerated, sure, but with at least an element of truth to them.

The worst part is, I have no idea which one he's in. The return stamp on the envelope is of some general social services office in Des Moines where the letters get routed through. And since I'm not family, they don't have to tell me. All I know is he's somewhere in the state of Iowa.

I read his last sentence over again. AJ rarely talks about his brother. The fact he even mentioned him in the letter means he's worried. But there's not a whole lot I can do. I could email Micah and get him to go check up on the guy, but I doubt Micah would travel to Ottumwa for that. Besides, who knows where Micah is by now? I haven't heard from him since his first email hinting at a prison escape. I finally replied to him a week ago, telling him how stupid it would be to attempt something like that. He's been ghosting me ever since, and I have no idea if AJ has had any contact with him.

I stare blankly out the window. The sun is shining, glinting off the metal barn roof, but I don't even notice it. I wonder for the hundredth time why I get a thousand chances, and AJ gets one. We did the same thing, yet ended up miles apart, in vastly different situations.

The corners of my mouth lift a little as I think of my new Saturday night obsession. AJ would be proud of me if he knew- breaking rules, having fun, and staying in control in whatever way I can. Too bad there's no race tonight.

A singsong chime breaks the silence, and I stuff the letter

under my pillow before racing down the stairs. In my haste, I almost trip over the pile of the laundry on the bottom step that I was supposed to put away earlier. I swing open the heavy wooden front door to see Chase and his two siblings waiting on the front porch.

Chase gives me a lopsided grin. "We made it."

His little brother Parker is having another painting session today, and since both Kate and Chase's mom are gone shopping, they decided everyone could come hang out here until they get back.

"Hi! I'm Rainey! And guess what- I'm five whole years old!"

The little girl is jumping up and down with excitement, her fair curls bouncing like coiled springs. She stops for a second and cocks her head to one side. "Are you Taz? I hope so! Chase says you're nice!"

Chase's neck gets red, and he ducks his head to avoid my eyes. He gives Rainey a push inside the door and kicks off his shoes.

"Do you know what else? My favourite chicken hatched five little chickens yesterday. They're so cuuute! And Buster- that's our dog- caught a chipmunk. He ate it all up, even the bones. I was sad, because chipmunks are so nice and cuddly."

"Um…nice, I mean, that's too bad," I say. Little kids, to me, are grosser and needier versions of the rest of us. I prefer either helpless babies who don't talk your ears off, or old people too deaf to hear what time you came in last night. How does Chase stand this child all day?

Chase, recovering from whatever made his neck go red, rolls his eyes at me and pretends to plug his ears.

"Is Madame Lemair here yet?" he yells over the top of his sister.

I shake my head. "She's running a little late," I yell back. "Her microwave broke this morning or something, and she needed to go pick up a new one."

I'm not sure how a broken microwave classifies as emergency enough to be late to a therapy session you're teaching, but Chase nods knowingly.

"Madame can't live without her microwave. She'd starve."

"Hasn't she heard of a stove?" I mutter under my breath.

A car pulls into the garage right then, and Parker changes expression for the first time. He's been sitting on the couch, avoiding everyone's eyes, but his face lights up as Madame enters the house. An oversize, bright red purse hangs off one arm. It matches her beret and tall, snakeskin boots. Her black wool dress comes to her knees, and when she leans over to give Rainey a kiss on each cheek, I'm afraid it might split over her sizable rear. Chase comes to stand by me, out of reach of Madame's exuberant displays of affection.

She puts a hand on Parker's cheek, and he looks her in the eye for a few seconds before focusing on her left shoulder.

"And how's my Parker today?" she asks, her tone as smooth as water over rocks. Now that's one voice I wouldn't mind listening to all day.

"Good, Madame." Parker's voice is soft, and low for a kid his age. He twists his hands in his lap. "How…are you?"

"Better now that I'm with you. Would you like to go work on your painting?"

He nods eagerly.

"When can I paint again?" Rainey pouts, feeling a little left out.

Madame smiles. "You know the drill, Rainey. In three quarters of an hour, you can come up. So…when the big hand is at the three, and the little hand is at the two."

Rainey stares at the big clock on the wall over the one couch and heaves out a sigh before slumping down over the armrest.

"Fiiiine," she grumbles. "I guess I could see the goats until then."

"You'd think the world was ending," Chase mutters in my ear as Rainey keeps pouting. "I guess since Rainey's happy on the couch, we can go play by ourselves," he goes on in his normal voice, giving me a mischievous grin.

Rainey pops up faster than a jack-in-the-box, eyes wide. "I wanna come too! I'm coming too!" she yells.

I almost wish she'd stay behind as she leads us outside, chattering all the way. No wonder Chase likes to come over and help muck out- goat bleating has nothing on the sound of this girl.

"I wanna go see the baby goats. They're my favourite," Rainey insists. She grabs Chase's hand and drags him to the mudroom. I follow behind reluctantly. I avoid the goats when at all possible unless they're outside in their little pasture. They don't smell so bad out there.

My eyes squish together as we step outside into the bright sunshine. Warmth radiates up from the dirt path as we head out to the barn. The weather this week is at a record high for April, following a massive thunderstorm last week. If it were up to me, I would be watching a show in the air-conditioned house. Rainey doesn't seem to mind the heat at all- she's skipping down the path like a rabbit.

"How many kids do you have?" she yells over her shoulder as she waits for us to catch up.

How old does she think I am? I don't have any- oh. Right. We're talking about goats.

"Uh…there are four goat kids right now. One doesn't have a name yet, and the other two are twins. They're names are Razzle and Tazzle. And Cairo of course, although he's not too little anymore."

Rainey giggles. "Did you name them?"

I shake my head. "Nuh-uh. I don't do names. There isn't a creative bone in my body."

Chase gives me a look. "You could if you wanted to."

Before I could figure out if that's supposed to be a compliment or an insult, Rainey's squeals distract us all. She runs to the pen with the babies. Cairo comes running to the gate when he sees us, wagging his little black tail, while the younger kids all shoot behind their mamas. I give him a scratch over the spot where his horns are starting to come up, and he gives a little bleat.

"This little guy will have to be moved into the next pen up before too long," Chase comments as Cairo leaves the gate to take a short spin around the pen, tripping over Razzle in the process. I bite my tongue to keep from protesting. I will not admit to forming an attachment with a goat of all things. If the stinky big goat pen is where they want him, so be it.

Rainey climbs under the gate and slowly approaches the unnamed kid. She's a little brown and white thing, only a day old.

When she reaches the far corner of the pen where the kid is lying, Chase turns to me and stuffs his hands in his pockets.

"So…how are you liking school so far?"

I shrug. "It's okay."

He shuffles his feet through the wisps of hay on the ground and stares out the grimy window at the end of the aisle.

"You and Talia are…hanging out a lot or what." It's not a question.

I sneak a glance his way, but he refuses to look at me. He doesn't look happy, though.

"So?" I answer, a little defensively. "Talia's nice."

"She's not a great person to be around," he mutters. He finally meets my eyes, and I'm the one who looks away first. He looks… concerned.

"Talia's fine," I mutter back. "Just because she wears a nose ring doesn't mean she's a gangster!"

"I never said anything about her looks. I know her family,

where she comes from. Trust me, she'll only drag you down."

Rainey glances over at us, and Chase quickly lowers his voice. He's mad, but it's nothing on how I'm feeling right now. I curl my hands into fists and turn on him.

"How about you stay out of my life? Last time I checked, I was capable of making my own friends," I seethe.

"And look where those friends got you!" he replies in a tight voice. "You have a chance here, and you're going to blow it by picking the worst possible option for a friend. You could do way better."

"Why do you even care? Go live your own life!" I spin around on one heel and am about to bolt for the door, but Chase grabs my arm. And he's strong. Wrangling goats and milking cows has put some muscle on him.

"Listen," he says through clenched teeth. "I know, because I saw what happened to my sister. She started hanging out with the wrong crowd, started drinking and partying and who-knows-what-else. And now she's gone. She hopped in a red pickup with some guy and rode off into the sunset, and I've never seen her since." He yanks a string over the top of his shirt and holds it in his palm. There's a bright pink cross dangling at the end. "That's why I wear this. Pink was her favourite colour, and I hope that wherever she is, God is watching over her."

I wrench my arm out of his grasp, still as mad as a hornet. "Well, your sister and I come from completely different places. Maybe riding off into the sunset is some disaster in your Jesus-freak household, but to me, it doesn't sound all that bad."

I storm down the aisle and out the door. The last thing I hear Chase say is, "You might have come from different situations, but you could still end up in the same place. And it isn't pretty."

What does he know about pretty places, anyway? He grew up in a barn, for crying out loud.

I stalk up the dirt path to the house and escape to my room.

I flop on my back across the cream duvet and sigh, the anger draining out of me. When I was younger, I always wanted someone to care about me. But now, I'm realizing how captive it makes a person. Also, since when does Chase have an older sister?

I pull AJ's now-wrinkled letter out from under my pillow and sit at my desk to scribble out a reply.

'Dear AJ,

Things aren't any better here. My next-door neighbour thinks he needs to parent me, there's a creepy painter who rents the attic, and the only thing I look forward to doesn't happen often enough. I may not be behind visible bars, but I'm a captive none the less...'

I scrunch up the paper and throw it in the trash. I sound like a brat. I tuck the letter into my desk so I can write a reply when I'm in a better frame of mind. AJ doesn't need to hear my complaints.

A soft knock sounds on the door.

"Who is it?" I mutter. If it's Chase, I'll be in jail for assault before supper.

"Rainey," a small voice answers. "I'm going up to paint. Do you want to come, too?"

I cringe, wondering if she heard me and Chase fighting.

"Chase won't be there," she adds in a conspiratorial whisper. "He's taking a walk in the woods."

Okay, yeah, she heard.

"Uh..." I'm almost embarrassed to be around her after the way I yelled at her brother.

Well, he started it. I won't let him stop me from having a little fun. If painting is fun...

"I'm coming," I decide, rolling off the bed. I open the door in time to see Rainey's face split into a beaming smile.

"Yay! We're gonna have so much fun!" She hops up and down.

"Ok, Rabb-uh, Rainey."

She turns around in the middle in the hallway and puts her hands on her hips.

"What were you gonna call me?" she asks sternly.

"Rabbit, cause you like to jump around a lot."

Rainey giggles. "I like that."

She sticks her butt out and proceeds to hop to the attic door, before jumping up each step with a loud thump. I take back my thoughts earlier about not being able to stand her as a little sister. Right now, I'd rather be with her than with her oldest brother.

Rainey barges into the studio and runs over to a miniature easel in one corner. The studio is full of sunshine from several skylights, and a small sink sits beside a wooden shelf full of canvases. A standing cupboard has small shelves, about four inches tall and two inches wide, filled with pots of every paint colour imaginable. Jars full of brushes line the top of the cupboard. Two large canvasses are sitting in the middle of the room.

Parker is putting the finishing touches on a small sailboat. The waves of a deep, dark ocean pound the craft relentlessly. I draw in a breath when I see his painting. It's incredible, from the foaming water to the dark clouds in the sky. An eagle is circling the boat, as though hoping to somehow summon the power to save the crew of the small vessel.

Rainey doesn't even look at Parker's picture, but heads straight to her own little station, where a half-finished painting of a few lopsided flowers is waiting.

Madame Lemair smiles and watches Rainey settle on the little wooden stool before turning to me.

"I guess when it's your brother, his paintings don't seem that special." So, she noticed my reaction.

"It's…amazing." I nod at Parker's scene.

"Parker has a gift with a brush. He's an extremely talented artist."

Madame gives him a fond smile. He doesn't look at either of us, but his face has a pleased look on it.

"Painting is one way Parker likes to express himself," Madame adds.

The dark-headed boy adds a final shadow to the sail of the boat before sticking his brush in a jar of water and spinning his stool around.

He cocks his head and glances at me for a split second before returning his gaze to the floor.

"I think I'll call this one 'Resilience'," he says in his soft voice.

"Why did you pick that name?" Madame encourages.

Parker risks another glance my way. I have a feeling this is something him and Madame usually do alone, and he's trying to decide if I'll laugh at him or not.

"That's a cool name," I say, hoping he'll continue. I'm dying to know why he's naming a storm-tossed ship 'Resilience'. I would have named it 'Imminent Death' or 'Doomed at Sea'.

"Well, you see…when I look at that boat, it looks so tiny in the waves. It looks like it could break apart any second. But it isn't. The boat isn't giving up and letting itself break apart. It's weathering out the storm. And that's resilience," he says, tracing a finger an inch above the wet canvas, along the boat's prow.

Wow. I wasn't expecting that.

"Your paintings are the best I've ever seen," I state honestly. I'm not an expert in fine art or anything, but I prefer this stuff over that famous painting of a lady with a harsh middle parting and wide shoulders- the Moaning Lisa or whatever it's called. I always thought she looked kind of ugly.

Parker grins at me. I'm ashamed to admit it, but I always thought autistic kids were kind of…I can barely say it, but I thought they were strange. I thought they couldn't do much or communicate at all. But Parker's not weird. He's the coolest kid I've met in a long time. Most guys his age are super annoying and gross, but he's polite, and sweet, and…resilient.

61

CHAPTER 8

Kate is down in the kitchen flipping pancakes when I get up. She's barefoot, and with her denim shorts and sleeveless plaid blouse, she looks like a regular farm girl. She smiles at me as I slide into my chair.

"So…" she starts, and I hold my breath, waiting for her to say something about Chase and me. He showed up a couple minutes before Kate and his mom got back from shopping, and we both refused to look at each other. I'm the type of girl who burns bridges and never looks back. If it's up to me, I'd much rather ignore him than apologize. I've learned that Kate is a perceptive person, so I'm guessing she knows something is up.

"I talked to one of your teachers yesterday."

Phew. No mention of Chase. But this doesn't sound much better.

I shrug, trying to act nonchalant. "Okay, so?"

Kate brings over a plate piled high with steaming pancakes and sets them down in front of me. My mouth waters at the smell.

"Mrs. Woodrow told me she's excited to have you in her class," Kate continues, plopping into her own chair.

I focus on my pancakes. Life is best when teachers and students ignore each other. This 'I enjoy having your kid in my class' stuff makes me feel weird. It's definitely not reciprocal.

Kate smiles. "She thinks you have a talent with a paintbrush. She mentioned you have some unique perspectives, and she's excited to see where you'll end up by the time school lets out."

School lets out in, like, a month. I don't think my painting techniques will have improved that much. As for 'creative perspectives'- well, I've done one project so far for her- a still life of an apple. She forced us to paint a fruit, and I'm not sure why an apple is such a unique choice. Maybe because I did a green apple instead of a red one?

"Mrs. Woodrow said she hopes you will take art again next year. She thinks you have a lot of potential," Kate adds when I don't respond.

I slap a hunk of butter on top of my pancakes and wish we would pray sometime in the next decade so I can eat. I never thought I'd be wishing for prayer- it's so awkward- but I need a way out of this one. Kate's compliments are sending my emotions into a tailspin. She's supposed to ignore me, ridicule me, anything but be this kind. I don't know how to deal with it.

"If she saw Parker's paintings, she wouldn't think anything of mine," I finally mumble.

"Well, very few people can paint like Parker." Kate laughs. "Don't compare yourself to him."

Finally, she bows her head and says a short prayer for the food before letting me dig in. I pour an obscene amount of syrup over my pancakes, like normal, and Kate rolls her eyes at me, also like normal.

Then she drops the real bomb on me.

"Your caseworker is coming today."

I choke on a bite of pancake.

"Moriah's coming today?" I squeak out between coughing fits. I've gotten kind of used to not seeing her. She never visits quite as often when I'm stuck out in the country. The fresh air threatens her sour disposition.

"I was thinking we should show her around the goat barn," Kate grins, eyes twinkling. "And I have the perfect shirt to wear.

It says, 'Jesus loves you, and I'm trying' across the front."

"Jesus might love her, but I'm certainly not trying," I retort. "Moriah Cade doesn't deserve anyone's love."

"Neither do I," Kate murmurs. She pushes back her chair and takes her cup to the sink. I shovel more pancake into my mouth and hope this conversation ends before it gets anymore churchy. I glance at the time and push my plate away. I love when Kate makes a big breakfast, but it frequently ends with me being late for school.

Kate soon hurries me out the door, and I slide into the truck seat with a sigh. This is going to be a fun Monday. I can't help but mentally tally up all the classes I'll have to endure with Chase across the room. It's tiring to studiously ignore someone you thought you liked.

At least with Moriah coming, I can skip retirement home duty after school.

* * *

I slide my brush across the canvas, leaving a wide blue streak. I scowl at the ridges left behind. Mrs. Woodrow is always telling us to tilt our brushes and make smooth strokes, but to me, all that fancy stuff is ridiculous. It probably works, though.

Ivan leans over from his chair and stares at my painting with a critical eye. He does that a lot. I guess he's decided he's my personal art tutor. His painting, some garish creation involving a six-legged frog and falling feathers, is disturbing. Somehow, he still thinks he's qualified to give me advice.

"You know, if you smoothed out some of those ridges, everything would blend better," he finally says. "And try adding another shade of blue into your sky to make the fade more gradual."

"I know," I grind out through gritted teeth. I'm in a bad mood today. Chloe keeps inviting me to sit with her and her friends at lunch, and I'm starting to run out of decent excuses so I can go with Talia instead. The only time I really spend time with Chloe is during math and history, and I think it makes her sad. But if she thinks I'm going to join her nice little cookie box of besties, she's sorely mistaken.

I turn back to Ivan and retort, "And your frog could use a bit more blending on his belly."

Ivan runs a paint-splattered hand through his short hair and looks at me in surprise. "It's not a frog, it's a Tricaderous. I recently finished a fantasy book about two kids trying to save the world from evil creatures called Gimlets. The Tricaderous was a surprising and unlikely ally whose incredible eyesight helped the heroes avoid attacks from the Gimlets on their quest to find the amulet that would destroy the Dark Kingdom's powers once and for all."

I should have known. Ivan looks rather boring and ordinary, but he lives in worlds that are light-years from the earth I live on. He's the only boy I know that reads five-hundred-page books in one sitting.

Ivan cocks his head and stares at his painting. "Does it really look like a six-legged frog?" he wonders, sounding worried. "The Tricaderous is described as having a scaly back, wide-set eyes, and a milky underbelly. He has the tongue of a snake and the face of an amphibious creature, but he isn't a frog, exactly. Maybe I should make his eyes a little larger…"

"It looks fine," I assure him. "Only a dumb, uneducated person like me would ever think it's a frog. And I did think it looked very *strange* for a frog."

Ivan sighs loudly and dabbles his brush in a dark, mossy green. I go back to making wide, sweeping strokes across my sky.

"What'cha making?"

The voice startles me, and my brush veers off in a wobbly line across the canvas, adding blue streaks to what was supposed to be a meadow.

Chase leans up against my table. He's got white paint above one eyebrow, and a dot of blue across one cheek. The artsy look is cute on him.

"Trying to make a meadow." So, did he officially break the silence? This is so weird.

His mouth twists around, like he's trying to hide a smile.

"Not everyone is a top-tier artist," I say defensively. If he came over to laugh at my picture, he can go right back to his seat beside Talia, who is watching us carefully right now, like a lioness ready to defend her cub.

Chase holds his hands up in surrender.

"Hey, it's pretty good. My paintings at the start of this class were horrible too. I mean, not saying yours is bad. It's really good…" I let him grovel around for a bit, trying to dig himself out of the hole he's made for himself.

"So, you do think it's horrible."

"No, I wasn't meaning it that way. My paintings were horrible. Yours are nice."

"Can it, Colby. You'll never get yourself out of that one," Ivan comments from his side of the table.

Chase's neck is turning red again. I decide to change the subject and try to put our argument behind us. For now.

"What are you painting?" I ask him.

"Oh yeah." He grabs hold of the lifeline, a man gasping for conversational air in a sea of words. "I'm painting a goat."

"A-a goat." The only criteria for this project was 'paint something you can relate to'. Ivan relates to fantasy animals, and I chose a meadow because I like wide open spaces and they're pretty. But a *goat?*

"Yeah. I got the idea from the series of sermons Pastor Evans has been doing on the prodigal. He started them the first Sunday you were at church, when he was talking about the story of the prodigal son. And yesterday he talked about the scapegoat. Don't you remember?"

I hadn't been listening. I do remember him going on about the Israelites, these people who lived thousands of years ago, letting a goat free with the sins of the people on its back or something like that. I thought whatever he was saying was weird, like something Ivan would read. This is honestly a weird conversation overall, but in this small town where everybody attends church, no one seems surprised.

"He said every one of us deserves to be a scapegoat, and be exiled for our sins," Chase prompts. "But Jesus was the Scapegoat for us."

"Yeah. Sure. Uh-huh. I remember," I lie. I need to get him to stop talking about this church stuff. It's too dangerous. Pastor Chris's last message came too close to breaking a hole through the protective walls around my heart, and AJ would tease me endlessly if he knew I will not be caught how close I've come to blubbering in public.

"So that's why I decided to paint a goat, because that's something I relate to," Chase finishes.

I still don't see a connection, but whatever. Ivan is absorbed in mixing the perfect shade of light green, so he won't rescue me. Besides, he goes to the Independent Church across town, so I'm guessing he doesn't have a clue what we're talking about.

Chase, apparently satisfied with that, turns and heads back to his table.

The bell rings before I'm done fixing the blue streak in my meadow, so I keep painting while everyone else packs up for the day. Within thirty seconds, most of the class has emptied out into the hall.

Soft footsteps cross the floor, and Mrs. Woodrow comes and sits in a chair nearby. I focus on painting a tiny pink flower. If I would have known she'd come talk to me, I would have ditched at the bell, ruined painting and all. I shift in my seat, trying to pretend she isn't sitting there watching me paint.

"Try holding your brush a hair to the left. it will help smooth those streaks a little better."

I dutifully tilt my brush and keep painting. Only two more strokes- then I can leave this place. The air is getting stuffier the longer Mrs. Woodrow watches me, and the walls seem to be closing in, inch by inch.

"That's a neat piece you're creating, Taz," she says after a moment. I wordlessly dab the brush back in the sage green and try to fix the corner of a large leaf that got vandalized by the blue.

"What made you decide to paint a meadow for this project?" she prods.

I shrug. "I needed to do something," I say.

I'm getting the feeling that Mrs. Woodrow missed her calling- she should have been a counselor. Or she's one of those people who thinks counselor and teacher are one and the same. I can almost see the mug in her cupboard with 'Nurturing Minds, Nurturing Hearts', scrawled across the front.

"Meadows always look so peaceful. It gives me a feeling of contentment."

I nod, but I don't get it. To me, meadows feel free and wild. You can't e backed into a corner in a meadow. There are no Mrs. Woodrow's in my meadow, either.

I swirl on the last bit of green and head for the sink to wash off my brush. Mrs. Woodrow finally decides the conversation is over, and heads for her desk. I finish cleaning up the rest of my supplies and race out the door.

"Bye, Taz," she calls. I throw a wave over my shoulder and keep jogging.

Wow, girl, you actually had a conversation with a teacher that didn't involve yelling, I congratulate myself sarcastically. I'm more comfortable with yelling teachers then with counselor teachers.

Kate is waiting for me near the soccer field, and I hop into the truck. We're halfway home before I remember who's planning to come after school.

"What time will Moriah be there?" I ask, trying to sound nonchalant. I'm not scared of her or anything, but it's always good to be prepared.

"She'll probably beat us home," Kate answers, giving me a sideways glance. I gulp in a mouthful of air and frantically think of ways I could somehow get the truck to break down. Kate reaches over and squeezes my knee.

"We'll be fine. Moriah can't do anything," she reassures.

Kate might be fine, but I know how much power Moriah Cade has, and she's not afraid to use it.

The familiar red Mini Cooper pulls in the lane behind us, veering off to the left after narrowly missing an oak tree. Finally, Moriah gets her vehicle straightened out and follows us right up to the house. The woman would park in the garage behind us if she could fit. The overhead door comes down before she makes any attempts, shutting us off from the sight of the platinum blonde case worker.

"Go put your backpack away," Kate suggests. "I'll keep Moriah occupied until you've at least gotten your school stuff organized."

I nod gratefully and hurry into the house. I hang my bag up in the closet and slip my shoes off, taking the time to straighten them on the mat before heading into the kitchen. If I can grab a snack before she gets in, I'll have an excuse not to talk. It isn't good manners to talk with your mouth full, after all.

The front door squeaks open as I slice through an apple. See, Moriah? I'm eating healthy.

Kate spies me in the kitchen and leads the Queen of Nasty herself over. Every staccato tap of Moriah's navy stiletto heels is like a gunshot on the hardwood floor. I keep my back turned and focus on cutting out the center of my apple halves.

"Well, well, Anastasia." It's more of a sneer than a greeting. I keep ignoring her.

"Are you deaf? I'm talking to you!" she hisses, her long fingers digging into my shoulder.

"Words are too precious to waste on those who don't understand them," I blurt out, surprising myself as much as anyone else.

Where did that come from? I wonder. Right- I had to look up inspirational quotes to paint on a canvas in art. Well, that was sure inspirational.

Moriah's nostrils flare open, the image of a horse in distress, and she glares at me.

"I can't believe you!" she spits out. "Have you no respect for authority?" She spins around and confronts Kate.

"I always said this child was going to work herself into trouble. If I were you, Miss Brighton, I wouldn't let this slip by! Who is she going to insult next, the President? If you like, we can terminate the placement immediately!"

My breath catches in my throat. Moriah Cade deserved every bit of what I said. Her job should be terminated if she can't handle kids like me. My attitude is the only thing I have left in this world. If Kate listens to her, I'm done. Finished. Doomed and defeated.

"It's a good thing I'm not you, then." Kate's voice could freeze a polar bear in a sauna. I've never heard her talk like this before. She's not mad- she's furious. "I will be reporting your unkind remarks to your office as soon as you leave, which I would prefer if you did now. A person in your position does not have the right to verbally abuse the minors placed in your care."

I'm silently cheering for Kate. Moriah's mouth opens and closes several times, like a goldfish gasping for air, but nothing comes out. Finally, she brushes past us to the door.

"Fine. If you are not happy with my services, I will leave as soon as I have given you the message I came here to deliver personally. But don't forget, I have a lot of power over where Taz gets to stay. And I am not afraid to use it."

I wouldn't have minded if she delivered her message by mail instead, but it probably gives her satisfaction to watch the colour drain from my face when she makes her next announcement.

"There have been certain, shall we say, suggestions lodged that a country property isn't right for you. You may not be at this place forever, Taz. Just saying."

Satisfied that she's ruined our day, she marches out onto the porch and slams the door behind her. The chandelier over the dining room table sways from the thud. I stare down at my toes as a deathly silence descends on the room. I could choke right now.

"Well," Kate starts. "Well. I guess that happened."

That's all she has to say? What about Moriah's threats? Doesn't Kate realize what that woman can do? She'll stop at nothing to get me into the dirtiest cell in the state of Iowa.

Kate comes over and stands in front of me, almost toe to toe. She ducks her head and looks into my eyes.

"Hey," she says softly. "Moriah can threaten you all she wants, but the truth is, it's just that- empty threats. I'll report this, and maybe she'll get moved or fired, maybe not, but either way, it's going to be okay. And as for moving- I can check into it, but it's the first I've heard about it. I'm guessing she thinks you're too happy here, and wants to get you out, but she's not the only one in power. That's not happening."

I bite my lip hard enough to taste blood and turn my head away. I am not going to cry in front of Kate. I'd rather go to juv- okay, no I wouldn't, but I can't cry.

I spin around and hurry out of the room. I know it won't be fine- life never ends up like that. It doesn't matter how much power Moriah has; she always finds a way.

CHAPTER 9

"You know, meeting up would be so much easier if you had a cellphone," Talia mumbles in a low voice.

I duck deeper into the shadows as a car passes.

"Had one a couple times. It always gets confiscated when I get caught again," I whisper back.

"They allowed to do that?" she wonders, giving me a look over her shoulder.

"Dunno. I'm usually not in a place to be questioning the rules when they take it. They're afraid I'll contact someone and run away again. So far, that hasn't helped, but whatever. I can survive without one. There are other ways to communicate." I let a bit of pride creep into my voice.

"Like snail mail?" Talia scoffs, ducking under a tree branch. The branch slips off her shoulder and almost whacks me in the face.

I don't answer her question. She knows I have my ways, and she'll ask eventually. I don't volunteer information, because information is power.

"Well?" Talia finally asks as our feet hit the pavement of the parking lot.

I let a small smile slip through. "I've become a master hacker. It's not that hard to get past a password into someone's desktop. Or you can use guest mode." Life skills from AJ. As long as Moriah doesn't find out, I'll keep doing it. And if she does find out, I'll find another way. I always have.

"Fair enough." Talia grunts. She leaves it at that, and we slip through the trees to our usual spot near the rim of the pit. As I sit down with my back against a tall oak, I can't help but imagine AJ here, cheering on the girl with the pink tips. He would love these races.

Sandy is back up in the truck bed. The music is pumping at maximum volume, drowning out the sound of revving engines as the bikers practice the course. Someone's added a new twist to the track- an old piece of culvert with the top half sticking up. Someone turned the sand around it into a large muddy mess, forcing the bikers to ride the slippery, sloped middle of the culvert.

I scan the bikes ripping up the course. Frog is in the lead, doing daring tricks and taking the corners at dangerous speeds. He seems to have recovered from his previous embarrassment. Smiley is right behind him, yellow tutu placed around his helmet instead of his middle, and the runner up from last week is going around the course backward, his orange hair streaming out behind him.

"Idiot," Talia mutters, waving at the guy. "Lena always has to pull dumb stuff like that for attention."

"Lena??" I ask, wondering if I heard right. The guy's name had never come up the other Saturday. "His name is Lena?"

"That's what we call him. His last name is Little, and he always leans his bike a little more than necessary for the corners."

"Lean-a Little. Very clever," I sneer. "What's his twin sister's name, I-Lean?

Talia shrugs. "Nah, that one goes by her real name, Cathy. Hey, I don't come up with the names."

I watch as Frog and Lena both roar toward the shortcut, Lena going up the hill and Frog trying to go down. For a second, it looks like they might crash halfway up, but Frog veers a little off the left at the last moment.

"Well, that was close," Talia drawls in my ear, but her nonchalant tone doesn't fool me. I heard her gasp.

"The Girl with the Pink Tips isn't here," I murmur as the bikers head off the track so the races can begin.

"If she comes, it won't be until the very end," Talia promises. "But she usually waits a few weeks and lets things settle down before showing up again."

"Fair enough," I answer. "Lena wouldn't like being beat twice in a row."

"Lena won't win tonight," Talia scoffs. "Bruno is here. He'll be the winner for sure."

She points out a big red bike with a tall, skinny Hispanic boy leaning into the handlebars. He has a purple headband around his forehead to keep his long, stringy black hair out of his eyes, and a tattoo of something along his jawline. I squint my eyes, and finally figure out it's a black and white rendition of a shrimp smoking a cigar.

"Bruno chose his own nickname. He's always dreamed of being the next Bruno Mars, and usually spends his evenings singing in bars until the customers kick him out. I've heard his voice described as a across between a cat fight and a screaming zebra, so I've never went to hear him. He's a good biker, though."

"Like they would let you in any bars anyway," I sneer.

"If I wanted to hear Bruno sing, I could get in," Talia argues.

Our friendly fight is interrupted by a dirty Ford with more rust than paint rattling up to the rim.

"Finally, we can get started," Talia sighs with relief. "Owen Bradley is always late."

Owen is the opposite of the last race's shark. His tree trunk legs are clad in ripped jeans and massive cowboy boots, and a plaid shirt strains over his sizable beer belly. He tips a stained cowboy hat at the crowd and opens the tailgate of his truck. He hops into the bed and unfolds a card table and a chair before plopping down and giving Sandy a thumbs up.

"And we're open for business," Sandy yells into the microphone, drawing a loud cheer from a dozen half-drunk teenagers.

The bikers draw spots, and the first guy pulls up to the starting line. Talia gives me a rundown on his family history, his nickname, and a thousand other details we both couldn't care less about. She likes having the leg up in knowledge.

Bruno draws the second spot, but a song by his hero comes on as he pulls up to the line, so he stops and dances to the whole thing. His long hair whips around his shoulders as he hops about like a rabbit on crack. Every time the chorus comes around, he opens his mouth and croons along, waving his arms wildly over his head. When the song ends and he finally gets back on his bike, the crowd claps and cheers. He waves exuberantly before nodding to Sandy.

Bruno's bike is a fiery blur as he whips around the course. He takes the jumps smoothly, and whirs around the corners at breakneck speed. Somehow, he still manages to stay in control. I hold my breath as he comes up on the new obstacle, the culvert. His wheels hit the curve of the pipe a little off center, and his bike starts to slip, but he gets it back on course and finishes the ride with a model jump over the rollers.

"Four-twenty-point-nine! Incredible time, especially with that new pipe!" Sandy cheers into the mic. The rest of the bikers visibly deflate. They're going to have their work cut to beat that.

The Girl with the Pink Tips still has a faster time, I note with satisfaction.

The next guy up, a bald man wearing a banana suit named 'Windy', feels too pressured to go fast. He completely misses the triple jump, and jounces over it. Angry at his time-consuming mistake, he pulls the throttle wide open and comes dangerously close to flipping as he sails around the clay pipe loop.

"He's not gonna have a good ride," Talia predicts ominously

as he bounces over a row of logs, sending a small metal piece flying off his bike.

"He needs to slow down," she mutters as he shoots down the drop off toward the culvert.

"He'll never-"

He finishes her sentence by misjudging the center of the culvert. His bike slides across the curving top of the pipe before flipping forward and launching its rider into the mud. His bike twists through the air and lands on his right leg, pinning him to the ground.

"I told ya," Talia mumbles as two of the other guys and Frog abandon their bikes and hurry onto the course. Sandy stays in the truck bed like a good host, staring blankly at the downed rider.

"Uhhhhhh," he groans into the mic, at loss for words. "Uh, welllll…"

Windy flops around in the mud, unsuccessfully trying to move the bike off his leg. Unfortunately, the force of the bike hitting the mud drove both it and Windy's leg a few inches down into the sand. It takes all three rescuers to pry the bike out of the muck.

Beside me, Talia creeps out from the edge of the trees, trying to see better. Everyone is too focused on the drama unfolding down in the pit to notice us, so we manage to slip close to the rim. Even from up here, Windy's ankle looks like a bloody mess.

"The front axle got him!" Frog yells up from the course, his foghorn voice carrying clearly through the night.

Two college kids make there way down and talk to Windy and Frog. Before long, the sound of a loud engine reaches our ears, and a third guy drives an old Ram truck down into the pit. Frog and one of the college guys help Windy to the truck. The two friends pile in after him, and they roar off into the night.

"They'll have to go all the way to Kalona." Talia grimaces. I don't have to ask for an explanation on why the hospital fifteen minutes away in Tripwater isn't good enough. I'm sure the cops are dying to bust this dirt bike ring. Talia told me once that the only reason they've never been up here is because everyone's forgotten about the place. If you don't know the way, you'll never find it. The road up here is little more than a logging trail by now, and its way farther by car than it is by foot- and its quite a walk. Walking into an emergency room around here in a banana suit with a bashed-up foot, especially when you're known to be 'one of them', would set off every sheriff's alarm in the county. Kalona is a good half hour away, so your identity is largely unknown. I hope he has the good sense to take the fruit suit off first.

The party soon resumes, with the next biker being much more cautious than Windy. Bruno remains a full three seconds ahead of everyone else, even Frog, who pulls a much better ride than last time. As I watch Bruno's satisfied smirk grow, I wish with all my heart that The Girl with the Pink Tips would show up and beat his time into the dust. He's strutting around, head high in the air, shot gunning beer after beer and catcalling the other riders as they come off the track. Owen Bradley looks a little miffed. With such a predictable winner, he's not making as much tonight.

Then a black object appears on the horizon. At first, I think it's my imagination, because according to Talia, she wasn't supposed to come tonight. But one look at Bruno's face says it all- a cloud passing over the sun couldn't steal the light from his expression as effectively as the small bike heading over the rim of the pit.

"She's here!" I hiss in Talia's ear.

Talia slides down onto her stomach, and I follow her, army-crawling to the rim until our noses are sticking out over the edge. Without any branches or tree shadows in the way, the pit looks bigger and brighter.

Sandy is stuttering incoherently in the truck bed. Owen

Bradley is almost bouncing in his folding chair, arms crossed and a satisfied smile on his face. I remember Talia saying it can't be the sharks putting the Girl with the Pink Tips up to this, but I'm starting to wonder. Even if they hate each other, it would make them enough extra money to be worth it and make it unpredictable. One shark can't control the girl, or soon everyone will be able to guess what nights she'll be out.

The bike doesn't slow down at all as it blasts past the crowd of guys gathered in a tight, frowning circle off to one side. Bruno leans against the side of the truck, arms crossed, as the black bike stops at the start line. He reaches up and taps Sandy on the leg, and the two converse in low tones.

"Are they going to let her go?" I whisper to Talia.

"They have to," she mutters back. "The rules are that anyone can ride. If they don't let her ride because they know she'll win, the sharks will go berserk. Everyone knows Owen Bradley keeps a .22 Magnum in his belt."

Sandy steps back into the center of the truck bed and holds up the timer around his neck. I watch as he presses the bottom a good second before yelling 'Go'. I'm pretty sure the girl rider sees it too, but she accelerates on the word. Knowing her, she'll still set records.

Her dark hair streams out behind her in a gentle wave as she flies towards the triple jump. She gets enough air to jump the clay pipe again, and her wheels spit up sand as she turns impossibly tight corners. It's like watching magic unfold all over again. I didn't think it was possible to top her last ride, but somehow, she's doing it. She slips down the drop off at a controlled slide, hitting the dirt right when the beat drops in the pounding music. For a second, it looks like her bike might wipe out, but she pulls up and recovers in time to get air over the speed bumps. Then she pulls up to the dreaded sunken culvert.

She's going way too fast. Windy wrecked at half her speed.

My heart is pounding in my chest. No one will rush to the aid of The Girl with the Pink Tips. And she'll never live down a mistake among this crowd.

But the girl must have eagle eyes, because her wheel hits the curving top of the culvert dead center, and she flies across without even a wobble. She jumps the dragon's back and steams across the finish line to the back of the crowd of bikers.

"Four-sixteen-point-seven," Sandy sighs into the mic.

"The culvert didn't slow her down much," I whisper to Talia. She grins.

The girl drives up beside the pickup and holds out her hand for the prize money. Sandy shuffles around the truck bed, as though he can't find it. Behind them, the other bikers are closing in in an ominous circle. I sneak a sideways glance at Talia. She's gone white around the ears.

The Girl with the Pink Tips tries backing up, creating more space against the crowd of angry men, but they press closer, using their bikes as a wall. She's trapped.

Miraculously, Sandy somehow 'finds' the money and holds it up, twenties sticking out of his fist.

"Is this what you're looking for?" he taunts, waving it in her face. She leaps up and makes a grab for it, but Sandy jerks his hand back at the last second. Around her, the biker crowd takes another step forward. The crowd on the rim shifts excitedly.

I clench my hands into fists and take a few shallow breaths. A fight is brewing, and for once, I care about the outcome. I don't want the mysterious girl rider to suffer.

A tall, heavyset man comes skidding to a stop beside Owen Bradley's truck and yells, "Cops! The cops are here!" The night explodes into a million red and blue bursts as a loud wailing sounds from the other side of the brick factory. Talia and I slither back into the safety of the trees. Owen Bradley dives for his truck, slamming the tailgate shut on his way by. The music pumps on, oblivious to the fear and adrenaline now charging the air. The bikers rapidly disperse, and roaring engines compete with pulsing sirens, each trying to drown out the other.

"Come on. Let's get out of here!" Talia whispers, tugging on my arm. The last thing I see as I turn to follow her is the Girl with the Pink Tips jump up and grab the stack of bills from Sandy's limp hand before hopping back on her bike and riding away.

Talia pulls me deeper into the trees, giving us a wide berth around the action.

"We gotta get out of here!" Talia whispers again, urgency creeping into her voice. She's right. I can already hear college kids heading our way, hoping to escape in the dark foliage of the forest. Coloured shadows bounce eerily through the leaves, lighting up running silhouettes.

My foot hits a rough, round object, sending me sprawling into the spongy earth. Talia hauls me back to my feet, and we continue our mad race down the hill back toward town. I can feel something wet running down one leg, but I ignore the pain.

The sirens get louder as we pass close by the parking lot of the old factory. The commanding shouts of police officers mix with the roar of a truck. Owen Bradley blazes his own trail through the scrubby undergrowth at the edge of the woods in a daring getaway. My heart rate accelerates as multiple pairs of eyes turn in our direction. One sight of me, and it's all over. I'm on my last chance. After what seems like an eternity, Owen's truck passes by, taking the stares with it.

My lungs are burning by the time we reach the soccer field where my old blue bicycle is lying. Talia collapses onto the grass, arms flung wide.

"Well, that was close." She wheezes.

I pick my bike up and lean against it, panting. My heart is pounding out of my chest, and a thin trickle of blood soaks the edges of a hole ripped into the left knee of my jeans.

"That was almost game over for me," I admit.

Talia stares up at me. "Whaddya mean?" she wonders.

I try to sound as nonchalant as possible, wiping the surprise from my face in an instant. Doesn't she know? What happened to 'news travels fast in a small town'?

"I've never managed to stay in one place, if you know what I mean," I tell her. "If I ditch Brighton's, I'm done. Off to places a little harder to run from." I don't tell her how much the thought of steel doors and iron bars scares me deep down inside. I may not be one to obey the rules, but escaping the consequences is high up on my priority list. For me, the repercussions are life changing.

"Anyway." Talia sits up, arms on her knees. "See ya in two Saturdays? Even if the races haven't relocated yet, I'm sure we can find something to do."

After the police raid, I'm not sure if I want to go out. But I refuse to be a chicken, even inside, so I push aside my nervousness and nod.

I hop on my bike and head off into the night, sticking close to the shadows until I'm out of town.

The gravel of the shoulder crunches under my tires as I leave Oakville behind. A gentle wind caresses my face, calming my racing heart and easing my anxiety. What I need right now is someone like AJ to laugh it off with. Talia might play tough girl, but the cop raid shook her up a lot. On the city streets, a raid is nothing. Out here in the sticks, the grandmas at church will know you were there by tomorrow. Your name will end up in the sermon as an example of what not to do.

I don't see the cruiser sitting at the end of Chase's lane until too late. The headlights are off, but the moon shines into the car enough that I can see the officer.

It's the cocky cop from Ottumwa. Why he's out here, far from his jurisdiction, at midnight, I may never know. We lock eyes, and time stands still for an agonizing second before I look away. I focus on pushing the pedals forward as fast as I can. My spine tingles, waiting for the tell-tale siren all the way down the road, in the lane, and up to the house. But it never comes.

"He's going to show up tomorrow morning," I mutter to myself nervously. Or maybe he won't say anything at all- Moriah Cade will appear on my doorstep one day with a court order.

I open the door as quietly as I can and slip off my shoes.

The light in the living room flicks on, and I jump out of my skin. Kate steps in front of me.

"About time you showed up."

"I-I was just taking a walk. I couldn't sleep." I muster up an excuse. Maybe I can pull the wool over Kate's eyes, like I did to Mrs. Cobalt after she caught me with a stack of cash under my pillow. She believed I had no idea how it got there, but Kate isn't buying my little story.

She gives me a hard stare and jerks her head toward the couch.

"Sit down. We need to talk."

I would rather swim across a pool filled with piranhas then hear what Kate has to say. But she leaves me little choice. I plop down on the couch and fold my arms across my chest. I can feel my heart pounding out a wild rhythm beneath my shirt sleeve.

Kate paces in front of the fireplace, rubbing her palms together as she walks.

"You and I both know you weren't out on a walk," she states calmly. "The question is, where were you?"

"Out with friends," I admit.

She turns to me, hands moving to her hips. "Who were you with?" she demands, her eyes squinting into slits.

"Chloe," I tell her, knowing Chloe is the role model of a perfect child.

Kate sits down beside me on the couch, and I scoot away

from her. She sighs and rubs a hand over her face.

"Taz, no matter what you did, you're in trouble. You broke the rules. But I'm not going to throw you out the door or shut you in the closet because of it. This is your home now, and you can't kick yourself out that easily."

"I was with friends," I stubbornly reply.

She chews on her lip and gives a quick nod.

"Alright. If that's how you want it, you're on chore duty every morning and night for the next three weeks. You'll have to be up by six tomorrow morning, so I suggest you head for bed and get some rest."

I give her a dirty look and trudge up the stairs, but I know I won't be sleeping for awhile. I can take yelling, screaming, and insults, but Kate's calm, steady approach is messing with me. For some reason, I *want* to like this woman. But my heart and head both know it's too dangerous.

CHAPTER 10

The goats are too loud for this early in the morning, and my eyes are still half shut with sleep. My shirt is sticking to my back, and my hair feels disgusting. The still air in the barn only compounds the smell, and it's shaping up to be another cooker today.

At least the church will have air conditioning.

Cairo sticks his little black nose out of the head rail and nudges my boot as I go past. I stop and give him a scratch behind the ears.

"You're the only one who isn't mad at me." I grin ruefully. Talia will be livid when she hears I got caught. Chase will have nothing to do with me, which is a bummer, and Kate has banished me to the goats twice a day. The animals don't seem too amused by the arrangement, either. They want their breakfast *now*.

My arms are burning by the time I throw the last loaf of hay to the billy goats, and my head is pounding from a scant three hours of sleep last night. I hope Kate is enjoying getting to sleep in for once, because I'm sure missing the privilege. I even contemplated ignoring chores this morning to see what would happen, but decided I shouldn't push my luck any farther. Kate has enough reasons to ship me back to Ottumwa as it is.

I peek in the kidding pen before heading for the house. I let the barn door slam behind me with a loud crash, and suck in a lungful of cool morning air. The gentle breeze feels good against my sticky skin. The weather and the sunrise are the only good things about getting up early- and too be honest, I wouldn't mind missing both to avoid the goats. I'm not cut out to be a farm chick.

Kate is downstairs in her sweats when I get into the house. She smiles innocently at me as I flop my stinky, sweaty body into a chair.

"How are the goats this morning?" she asks sweetly. I glare at her and don't bother answering.

"If you shower quickly, you can finish before the pancakes are done," she adds.

I drag my way up the stairs. I don't think humans are meant to work so early in the morning. I'm ready for a nap, and the day has barely started.

I pull together a decent outfit that isn't too wrinkled. I've started to dress up a little more for church, to keep Mrs. Bennitt and the rest of her quilting club from whispering about me in highly audible 'quiet' voices. Apparently, I'm a street urchin, a misplaced child, and a runaway of the worst kind, among other things. I've heard stuff about myself from them that I didn't even know about.

I won't let them control my whole life. I grin to myself as I pull out my bright red Converse to complete the sickeningly proper outfit. AJ would be proud, and besides, Mrs. Bennitt's quilting club would die out if it weren't for my antics.

I run through the shower at record speed. When I get out, I don't smell the pancakes yet, so I sneak into Kate's office and log into the computer. A new notification pops up. I click the email icon and open the message.

to: taz4ever
from: micdawson
subject: re: the bro

i gotcha. aj is in casings outside of fort dodge its
a building in the hicks bunch of fields is all thats
around. bro isnt doing great in there but if there's
ever a chance to get him out we will.

M

"Taz! Pancakes are ready!"

Kate's voice makes me jump. From the sound of it, she's standing at the foot of the stairs. I hastily log out of the computer and yell back. The office is beside the bathroom, so hopefully she won't figure out where I am.

I run down the stairs and slide into my chair. Kate bows her head, and I follow suit, but I keep my eyes open, because who's going to know? Besides, I feel like not praying is better than pretending to pray, like I might be struck down with fire if I pretend. It seems Kate is getting a bit of a conscience into me, after all.

"Careful not to spill any syrup on your dress," Kate cautions as I dump half the pitcher on my pancakes. I roll my eyes at her.

"I'm fourteen," I moan. "I'm not a baby."

"If you're not a baby, are you going to man up- or, I should say, woman up- and tell me where you were last night?"

So, this is how it's going to be- every conversation is going to turn into a lecture.

"I already told you- I was out with friends."

"So where did you go?" is the next question.

"We went to a rodeo and tried mutton-busting," I answer sarcastically.

Kate's quiet for a moment. She likes to do that before dropping a bombshell. I brace for impact, and sure enough, the explosion is a big one.

"Did you hear about that dirt biking ring that got busted up at the old brick factory? Apparently, some guy got hurt, and then he went through a ride check on his way to the hospital in Kalona, and the cops figured out where he was coming from. They got there just in time to break up a nasty fight, too."

She's watching me closely, and I have to work hard to keep all expression off my face. How does she know?

I shrug. "Didn't hear about that. I don't watch the news."

She gives me one last, long look before turning back to her pancakes.

After that encounter, I'm not looking forward to being stuck in a truck with Kate, even for the five-minute drive to church. She's done talking, though, and cranks some worship songs all the way there.

The hot, surfer type youth pastor is the greeter again today. The girl in front of us is flirting hard with him, earning jealous looks from a few others and exasperated nudges from her mom. She's holding up the line, fawning all over Daniel or whatever his name is. She compliments his hair, and how well his white button-down matches his khakis, and the program he did three weeks ago for the kids at the local homeless shelter, which I'm almost certain she never attended. The youth pastor's smile is getting stiffer by the second, and he nods gratefully when the girl's mother finally manages to pry her daughter away.

His smile is still a little too bright for my taste when he greets us, so I give him a cool nod and a short handshake. It seems guys like him get so much attention they come to expect it, even if they don't always like it, but Taz Robbins will not be done in by a youth pastor, even one from Myrtle Beach.

Kate isn't in the mood to talk much either, so we both escape to our pew. Chase grins at me and waves as he follows his family across the aisle. I half-heartedly wave back. After the morning I've had, I'm in no mood to be nice to anybody.

After a singing a slow song about lost sheep that could put anyone to sleep (the song, not the sheep), the brown-suited bean pole of a preacher gets up and sets his Bible on the pulpit. He massages his forearms as though they're tired from lugging the heavy Book around. His noisy throat-clearing is my sign to slip off into a daydream.

"From my almost fifty years of experience, I have come to the conclusion that there are two types of people in this world- runners and fighters."

I sit up, and my eyes stop sliding shut. He may be over thirty years my senior, but what gives him the right to classify us all into two categories?

"Runners dodge the light, chase the shadows, and get out of there at the first sign of real trouble. They disappear when someone gets too close, afraid of getting hurt. Runners don't stick around when the going gets rough. They're like the prodigal son- they'd rather face the pigs all alone than face the music at the mercy of another human being.

"Fighters, on the other hand, boil over and lash out. They stand their ground and are ready to take down giants ten times bigger than themselves. Fighters, like the apostle Peter, will cut off ears if needed. They'll fight to the death."

I need to stop listening now! I tell myself. This guy is getting close to the truth, and as a preacher, I'm sure he has things to say that I don't want to hear. I don't have to think too hard to figure out which one I am- my record proves it.

"Both have something in common, however. Running away and fighting the situation both stem from a need for control; because if I'm in control, I can't get hurt, or at least not as easily."

He pauses and clears his throat again, taking a sip of water from a cup nearby before continuing.

"I know which one I am, and you probably know which one you are. The reality is, our pasts often define our present actions. I still have the tendency to duck and run from trouble because of things that happened in my childhood."

Isn't it an unspoken rule of preaching to never tell a personal story unless it sheds you in a good light? Yet this guy has beads of sweat on his forehead, so I don't think he has a nice Sunday morning story for us. I can't shut my eyes and ears now. I'm too intrigued.

He swipes an arm over his brow and grips the pulpit with both hands.

"When I was four years old, my mom taught me to run to the couch and hide under it every time my father came home late from work. I'd lay on the threadbare carpet with the designs pressing into my cheek as Dad stumbled into the house. I could picture my mother sitting on a kitchen chair, trembling, waiting, until he found her. It always started the same- he'd ask her where his supper was. She'd take the covered dish off the warming plate on the stove and set it on the table in front of him. He'd eye it suspiciously for a moment before turning on her in a fit of rage.

"'I work all day to support you and the kids,'- there were seven of us- 'and you can't even have a fresh meal waiting for me?' he'd shout.

"'I-I wasn't expecting you home so late,' she'd stammer back. 'And the kids were hungry.'

"'Those stupid kids can wait! I make the money around here! This stuff tastes like junk when it's been sitting around for half an hour on the stove!'

"He'd poke a finger in. 'And it's not even WARM anymore!'

"At this point, my dad was out of control. Combined with the liquor he'd had after work, he was a tangled, violent mess of wrath. I would scrunch up in a ball, with my hands over my ears, wincing at every ensuing slap of skin on skin. My mom would start off with whimpers, which escalated to choked screams, before dying down into the oblivion of unconsciousness. The door slamming shut behind my father was my signal to creep out from behind my protective hiding place and assess the damage.

"By the time I was six, the drunken beatings were happening so often that new bruises layered the old before they had time to heal. My oldest sister, thirteen at the time, dropped out of school to take care of the house, because my mother had become too broken to do it. My second sister finally called the police one day when my father attempted to strangle my mom. They put my dad in custody, where he remains to this day. My mom was sent to the hospital with a broken collarbone and a concussion, and us kids were split up in foster care. My mom died a year later from a drug overdose. We didn't learn of her passing until three years after.

"My father never physically harmed any of his children, but his emotional beatings remain with me today. For years, I would jump every time a door slammed. While my youngest and only brother was a fighter in every sense of the word, I ran. Where he lashed out, I crawled inside of myself. While my brother fought back at the world, I hid from it. I rarely spoke, at least not voluntarily, and during the two years I spent on a family farm, I walked the back fields for hours, circle after circle. I would have nightmares that wouldn't leave until I physically exhausted myself. I used to run laps around the house at midnight."

When the pastor stops for another drink, the congregation falls into dead silence. I sneak a glance at Kate. She's riveted to the speaker. Well, so am I. I feel his pain. I was unwanted, too- sent into foster care at age three because my mom preferred drugs to her child. And as for my dad- I don't even know his name. I bite my lip against a wave of emotion. Maybe this preacher guy knows what he's talking about, after all.

"At age eleven, I was fostered and then later adopted by a Christian family who lived near Des Moines. I took their last name and became one of theirs- at least in theory. But on the inside, I was still afraid of any relationships. They talked about a God Who loves each of us, and how they loved me, and how I belonged."

Here goes, I think. I knew there had to be a God moment in there. Now would be a good time to start thinking about…oh, how about dirt bikes?

But when he continues, I'm still listening, whether I like it or not.

"I wasn't buying it. In the world I'd known, love didn't exist, except in the form of a mother pushing us away so we could be safe. Love came with guilt- why didn't I stand between my parents? This might have all been avoided, if only…"

You could have heard a grain of wheat hit the floor as the pastor pauses and looks out over the congregation. His sweeping gaze locks on my mine for a split second, and I get the feeling he understands what it's like to be me.

I shrug that thought away. No one understands what it's like to be me, except maybe AJ. And Talia- she gets me.

"For years, I shunned God. I chose friends my new parents wouldn't like. I was 'sick' on Sundays more often than on all the other days of the week combined. I was into alcohol and started experimenting with drugs by age fourteen. Then, at fifteen years old, when I felt I was in so deep I couldn't get out if I tried, I met God face to face on the R63.

"It was three in the morning. I was drunk, without a license, in an unfamiliar car. I needed a ride home, and my buddy was even worse off than I was. We figured we'd crash at his place- his parents weren't home- and I would straggle on to my place the next day to face the music from my parents.

"There's a slight curve in that road before the turnoff onto

Dubuque Street, which is where my friend lived. I was going way too fast, and barely made the curve before almost blowing past my friend's road. I turned a sharp right, and the tires rolled across the pavement for a few seconds before the vehicle spun completely out of control. We careened off the road into a small stand of scrubby trees. I watched the windshield cave in before it finally registered in my addled brain that I should take my foot off the gas. The hood crumpled over us, trapping us both inside the car.

"Sitting there, awake but completely encased by folded metal, listening to the groaning of my unconscious and more deeply wounded friend, I couldn't run. I wanted to. Every particle of my being told me to scram before the cops got there. I'd have time- my phone was lost somewhere in the wreckage, and our only hope of rescue was some passerby who happened to see a car in the trees on this lonely country road.

"We waited two hours before rescue came, in the form of a middle-aged woman whose headlights picked up our vehicle at just the right angle. She was a nurse, coming home from her hospice patient's house. Those were the longest two hours of my life. My friend slipped in and out, but I was conscious the whole time. And while I don't remember every single minute of it, I do remember praying voluntarily for the first time in my life.

"Because when you're forced to stare life in the face, you realize there must be Someone bigger out there. There must be, or else there's no way you're getting out of this on the winning end."

He glances at the clock at the back of the building. I crank my head around and follow his gaze. I stare, unbelieving, at the numbers. How is it this late already? I don't think I've ever focused on one thing for this long in my entire life, unless it involved flashing lights and loud noises.

"That night changed the course of my life forever. There were many moments afterward when I wanted to run, but now I had a reason to stay. That's the difference that Jesus makes."

He looks at the clock again and closes his Bible.

"You can run, you can fight, you can try to get out, but eventually you're going to come face to face with your circumstances, in a situation where you can't make it out alone. God is trying to get your attention. Don't make it take a car crash to do it."

With those cryptic words, he leaves the pulpit.

As we stand up for a closing hymn, my mind is swirling with a funnel cloud of thoughts. *God is trying to get your attention. Don't make it take a car crash to do it. You can't run forever.*

I push them all aside. What does this preacher know, anyway? I know tons of people who don't buy into this religion stuff, and they're still standing.

A twisting wave of emotion rises in me, one I've felt countless times before. I need to get out of here.

As soon as the song is over, I slip out of the pew and head for the back of the building. I ignore Chase, who's trying to get my attention, and brush past Mrs. Bennitt and the half dozen old ladies crowded around her, chattering excitedly about Mr. Wiley's toe fungus. As I head for the door, I see the pastor standing off to one side alone, and suddenly, I need to know. I hurry over to him.

"Sir, what happened to your friend?" The question is out before I stop to consider that he might not want to share.

But the creases and wrinkles around his mouth smooth out into a quiet smile.

"My friend's name was Charles. His life turned around that night as well, and he went on to become a successful man, both in his family and in his community. In fact, one of his children is here today- Kate Brighton."

"W-what?" I stammer. This is all eerily connected. How come

I never heard about this? Although I guess, 'By the way, Taz, your 'grandpa' was in a car crash as a teenager' doesn't fit in any of the superficial conversations that Kate and I have had. I remember the strong, smiling man on the canvas upstairs in the hall. I can't imagine him as a young, reckless teenager.

The pastor nods. "Charles went home to be with the Lord three years ago, but his impact in the community will stand for years to come."

I nod my thanks to the pastor and abruptly turn away. I need to get out of here.

CHAPTER 11

I fold the purple sticky note into quarters and thrust it deep into my pocket before slamming my locker door shut. I start down the hall, but a shout makes me pause.

"Taz! Wait up!" Someone grabs my shoulder, and I twist away. I turn around to see Chloe, her orange curls bouncing on her shoulders. I paste a smile on my lips. Despite her being the first friendly face here, we never got around to hanging out much. We share answers in math- my strongest subject- and copy notes from our neighbours in history, a subject neither of us enjoy. But ever since I started sitting with Talia for lunch, it seems like a friendship with Chloe can't happen. Everyone avoids Talia like the plague. In a town so overwhelmingly 'Christian', I would have thought 'love your neighbour' would be prevalent. But apparently that verse only applies to people who will be a good influence on you. We don't help the rebels around here. We cast them out.

"How's it going?" Chloe vibrates with energy. She takes two hopping steps for every one I take, and constantly switches from walking backward in front of me to dancing beside me.

"Good. You?" Besides the fact that she's acting like a Mexican jumping bean.

"Amazing! We had a test today in English on prepositional phrases, and I aced it."

"Prepa- what?" I sputter. I've always hated English. My English teacher the first semester at my other school was tall, built like a pro wrestler, and had exactly eight wiry hairs protruding from her chin. She yelled a lot, pressed so hard on the chalk she fused it into the blackboard, and whacked you on the head with her ruler if she caught you sleeping, which I'm pretty sure is illegal. I don't think I learned a single bit of educational knowledge in that class.

"Prepositions. Like about, above, into, before..." Her voice trails off as she looks at my blank face. "You really don't know what a preposition is?"

"I don't care what a preposition is," I snap. Her smile wavers for a second, and I would feel bad except I can't have her teaching me on lunch break.

"Okay," she says, brushing it off as we enter the noisy cafeteria. Talia calls it the pig pen, and I agree with her. It's loud, dirty, and unmannerly, and they feed us slop.

"Anyway, I was going to ask you if you want to come to my house on Saturday night for a sleepover. We could have a barbecue by the pool, sleep outside on the deck, and then go to my church on Sunday." Chloe gives me a hopeful look.

I bite the inside of my lip and remember the note in my pocket. 'I HAVE AN IDEA', it says, written in giant block letters. There's no signature, but I know exactly who gave it to me. She's watching us right now from across the cafeteria, patiently waiting for me as I scramble to come up with an excuse. Saturday nights stay open for our little adventures. But I also don't want to hurt Chloe's feelings more than I already have. She's trying so hard to be my friend.

"Um, well, I could come for the day to swim or something, but I have to do chores in the evening," I blurt out. I give myself a mental pat on the back for that one. It will solve both problems, and it's actually true. I *do* have to feed goats- it's my punishment.

Chloe's face falls for a second before lighting up again. "Kate will let you off chores for one night, no?"

"Well, it's kind of a punishment, so…" I let my voice trail off and duck my head, trying to act embarrassed so she won't ask more questions.

"That's too bad," she says, and lets the subject go as we approach the counter. "But it'll still be fun if you can come for the day to swim. Saturday is supposed to be a cooker. I can't believe it's so hot already. It's only the first week of May." She moans as the lunch lady plops a generous scoop of something that looks like mutated banana guts onto her tray. The sign says Mac 'n' Cheese is on the menu today, but this is no Mac 'n' Cheese.

Chloe gets hung up in the line over her dessert choice, so I take my chance and head across the cafeteria to Talia. I sit down across from her and let my tray fall to the table with a clatter.

Talia smirks at me. "I was excited when I saw the menu today, but then I saw the food. Whoever wrote up the menu must have misspelled something."

I nod ruefully. "At least it will taste good," I say, picking up my fork.

As unappetizing as the food always looks, it usually tastes normal. I put a forkful of the cheesy glob into my mouth before pointing my utensil at Talia.

"So, what's with the note?"

She feigns ignorance. "What note?"

I give her a mock glare and pull the rumpled purple paper from my pocket.

"This one."

Talia nods and a little grin works its way out of her. "I have an idea," she says.

"I couldn't tell," I mutter sarcastically.

Talia's smile grows. "I have a plan to find the Girl with the Pink Tips."

I raise my eyebrows skeptically, but inside I'm getting excited.

She must live somewhere, and she has to eat, and shop, and fix her bike.

"So, what's the plan?" I ask after a sufficient pause to hide how eager I am.

"The library."

I choke on my macaroni. I doubt Talia has ever set foot in a library before. I'm surprised she even knows what that word means.

"There's this thing called Iowa License Plate. If you pay for a membership, you can look up records for every vehicle in Iowa. And I know the local library has an account on their computers, because the auto class went there last semester to practice reading VIN numbers."

I don't ask Talia how she knows all this. For a girl without many friends, she has a wealth of information about everyone and everything.

"Once we know her name, things will be a whole lot easier," Talia adds.

I raise an eyebrow at her. "Do you know her license plate number? Does her bike even have one?"

"Yes, and yes. I memorized it the other night."

"You should meet my friend AJ sometime. You two would hit it off," I say with a grin.

She cocks her head to the side. "That would be cool."

I brace for the questions to follow, about who he is and where he is and when she can meet him, but they don't come. My respect for Talia grows as she leaves the subject in my control.

I scrape the last bit of cheese off my plate and stand up. "Anyway, what are we waiting for? Let's get to the library."

Talia laughs. "We'd better go now before the bell rings. There are teachers roaming the halls looking for skippers during classes. We'd have to go through the furnace room to get out then."

We leave our trays on the table, against cafeteria rules, and run for the door, hoping to escape before the lunch ladies notice and call us out. I cast a discreet look over my shoulder as we near the exit and meet Chase's eyes from across the room. His expression is dark, and we hold eye contact for a few seconds before I turn back around.

"You are not in control of my life, Chase," I mutter under my breath. "Even if you think you are."

"Did you say something?" Talia calls over her shoulder as she navigates the halls at warp speed.

"Nothing," I call back, jumping the obstacle course of legs from sprawled out students relaxing in the hall.

Talia throws open the metal side door with a ferocious clang, and we burst out into the fresh spring air. Dark clouds roll across the horizon, and the air holds the still, heavy warning of a thunderstorm.

"For a place that's known for wild storms, we sure haven't had many this year," I say, looking up at the churning mass of gray.

"We'd better hurry to the library before it rains," Talia answers, breaking into a run again.

We take the back way, circling behind the dumpsters and onto the sidewalk by the old Presbyterian church-turned-art-hall. Thunder rumbles in the distance as we cut through an alleyway onto Second Street. A few large raindrops splat down on my arms as we run past the flower shop and an old gray house that's now a hair salon. The rain begins to fall in earnest as we head up the wide cement steps of the old, red brick library. Talia pulls open one of the large, solid oak doors, and I rush in behind her. The door closes behind us with a soft whisper.

We wipe our feet on the intricately woven mat right inside the building before ducking through another set of doors into the main library. The dark walnut desk off to the right is empty, and I can hear faint murmurs floating from somewhere in the maze of bookshelves. Rows and rows of dark wood cover almost every inch of floor space, except for a row of desks off to the left. Talia heads in that direction.

"Can I help you, ladies?" a pleasant voice asks a moment before we reach the computers. A tall, elegant woman in a long dress with small daisies scattered across it appears from behind a shelf, a heavy volume in her hand. A tag clipped to her dress front reads Mrs. Comet. I eye her thin frame and swept-up gray hair and wonder how fast we could immobilize her if needed. We'd have to do it quietly, though.

"We're fine, thanks," Talia says, giving the woman a charming smile that I've never seen before. "We need to look something up for a school project."

"Doesn't the school have its own computers?" the woman wonders, a suspicious look crossing her otherwise pleasant face.

"We need to use one of the programs that isn't available on the computers at school. You do have the newspaper archives online, right?"

The woman relaxes and smiles again. "Of course. We recently updated the archive program as well, so it should be even easier to find what you're looking for. Let me know if you need anything." With that, she spins on her heel and meanders off into the labyrinth once again.

Talia winks at me as she slides into one of the black leather chairs. "That was too easy. She's a sharp old tack, and I thought she might be a bit of trouble."

Her fingers fly over the keyboard as she navigates to the right website. The sign-in prompt is auto-filled with the library account's information.

Talia types in a series of letters and numbers into the search bar. "7974 AF… enter," she mumbles to herself. I hold my breath as the screen loads.

The outline of a dirt bike pops up.

The license plate 7974 AF is registered to a 2022 KTM

300XCW TPI in Iowa… Talia clicks the 'View Owner' button before I have a chance read the rest of the blurb, and we wait anxiously for the data to load. It's the longest thirty seconds of my life.

A list of information pops up, and Talia scrolls past the vehicle specifications and maintenance reports to the owner records. I lean over her shoulder.

"It's registered to one Miss Sara Geiger," Talia announces triumphantly.

"Do you know anyone around here named that?" I ask.

She shakes her head. "Nuh-uh. But we can look in the white pages. I'm pretty sure they're online, too. No one uses phone books anymore."

A quick google search takes us to the Iowa white pages, and Talia enters the name of the mystery driver. The page comes up with nine results, and we quickly scroll through them.

"She's in Des Moines… won't be her. This person isn't even in Iowa, dunno why she's on here… there. Sara May Geiger, 1510 Misty Lane in Staten. That's a tiny collection of houses about ten miles east of here, that somehow got its own name."

I rummage through my backpack and find a scrap piece of paper and a pencil to scribble the address on. There's no phone number listed, but Talia is searching farther into the mysterious Sara's life, checking for a criminal record.

"There's nothing," she says at last, exiting the site. "No criminal record, no spouse, no family listed, nothing. Everything comes up empty."

"Would all that stuff even be on some random website?" I ask. "I mean, some people could use this information for some pretty messed up stuff."

"Usually, it will come up with something," Talia answers, making me wonder how many times she uses this kind of thing. For all I know, she's a master harasser. "It doesn't always give all the details, but it will at least say 'criminal record found' or something. But there's nothing here."

Talia tries searching the web for Sara Geiger and comes up with a host of results, none of them likely to be the Girl with the Pink Tips, unless she has a side career as a pastry chef in San Antonio.

"Try 'Sara Geiger dirt biking'," I suggest.

Talia types in the keywords, and a name pops up on the screen.

"There's a Tara Geiger who's some famous motocross driver," Talia says, scrolling through an article.

"Are you sure you got the name right? Maybe the sharks hired this Tara person to beat everyone," I offer, but I'm skeptical of that idea. I saw the screen- the name was Sara.

"I'm sure I got the name right," Talia mutters. "And I doubt the sharks could convince a legit motocross legend to come to a one-horse town and compete in a race that's barely even a race. This gal's an expert. The build is similar, though."

"How hard is it to change your name?" I ask, suddenly struck with an idea.

Talia spins around in the chair and raises an eyebrow at me. "Not hard. Why?"

"Maybe the Girl with the Pink Tips changed her name recently. That would explain the lack of records. And when she changed it, she decided to name herself after one of her heroes- a motocross legend."

"You might be on to something there," Talia grudgingly admits. "But if we have her address, we don't need all the other stuff. The sharks are working on preparing another track, but it won't be ready for a few weeks. Wanna meet up this Saturday night for a little spy mission?"

"I'm down." I grin.

How am I going to last through four more days until then?

CHAPTER 12

Micah was right- Casings Juvenile Detention Center is in the middle of the country, surrounded by fields. There's a house down the road, according to Google Maps, and I wonder if its inhabited. Would anyone want to live beside a detention center? I've seen people give a wide berth to kids who are on mandatory community service, which is me right now, unfortunately. 'Granny Work', we used to call it- picking trash out of gutters and weeding the park flower beds.

I switch the map settings to satellite and zoom in on the property. There are two buildings; one is a small office, and the other is a four-story brick and steel structure that looks like a school, except for the barred windows and deadbolts. A tall, metal fence and several loops of barbed wire encircle the buildings, a cracked basketball court, and an acre of scraggly weeds. A rusted swing set sits abandoned outside the fence, taunting the inmates that this place was once full of happy children and colourful artwork.

I exit the computer and pad softly back to my room, the latest envelope from AJ in my hands. Kate is out with the vet, checking a sick goat, and Chase left after helping us muck out this morning. He had an emergency splinting job to do. Rainey's favourite chicken got its foot stuck under a log, or something like that. Madame Lemair and Parker will be busy painting in the attic for another hour, so I have the house to myself.

I rip open the envelope and slide the single sheet of lined

paper out. It's folded into quarters, and the ink is smudged, like someone had sweaty hands when they read it. I immediately noticed that some of the words are whited out.

Dear Taz,

Things could be better down here. One guy got taken out by a ———— the other day. He's kind of messed up. We're all kind of holding our breath, wondering who will be next. There was a ———— the other day. I think that's what triggered it. He had to go by ambulance to ———— Hospital.

Jack isn't doing well, either. The reports aren't good. My aunt is into some stuff, if you know what I mean. I worry about him.

I wonder how much longer I'll be in this place. My trial date keeps getting pushed out. I know I'm guilty, but isn't there alternative service a judge could give me instead of this? A guy loses hope in a place like this.

Keep the letters coming. They're the only good thing in this place.

AJ

I hold the letter up to the window to see through the white out. The sun isn't bright enough to get through, so I run downstairs to grab a flashlight.

Kate's cellphone chimes from its face down position on the kitchen counter. I pick it up and stare at the caller ID.

"Child Protective Services. No way I'm answering that," I mumble. I change my mind at the last second. If Moriah's coming for another visit, I want to be forewarned. Kate likes to wait to tell me, because she thinks I'll worry, but I'd much rather be able to prepare in advance.

"Hello, Kate speaking," I say, hoping the phone will distort the voice enough no one will catch on.

"Hello Kate, this is Angela Turner from Child Protection

Services Iowa. Do you have a minute to chat?"

"Of course! How are you doing, Angela?" I answer, trying to infuse friendliness into my voice. I clench my shaking fingers into a fist and press the phone harder into my ear.

"I'm good, thanks. I'm calling to inform you that your social worker, Miss Moriah Cade, has been assigned to other duties. Your new social worker, Miss Bailey Rand, will be by in the next week to meet with you and pick up where Moriah Cade left off. Please let us know if there are any concerning incidents regarding Miss Cade where retribution may be provided. Do you have any questions?"

"Uh, no," I stammer out. "Th-thanks for letting us know." I valiantly try to recover my 'Kate voice' for the final good-bye and fail miserably.

I set the phone back down on the counter and stare at the blue teapot on the stove.

Moriah's not coming back. It finally sinks in, and I throw my hands up and dance around the kitchen.

"She's gone!" I shout. "She's gone! No more Moriah!" I need to write a letter to AJ right away. This will brighten his day.

"What's going on?" Chase steps into the kitchen and quirks an eyebrow at me. I sheepishly lower my hands. I can feel the heat creeping up my neck as he stares at me in bewilderment.

"When did you sneak in?" I ask shakily.

"I finished with the chicken leg, so I decided to come back over, but… I didn't mean to interrupt your dance party."

My face feels like it's on fire, and I look down at my toes.

"No, it's…fine. I got some good news."

"No kidding. Something about a Moriah?" He gives me another questioning look. "Hey, isn't that the name of your social worker?"

"Uh, yeah. She got moved to a new department or something, so I'm getting a new social worker."

He raises his eyebrows and whistles. "Whoa. That *is* good news. Do you know who the new one will be?"

"It's someone I've never met before. All they said is that she'll come sometime in the next week."

The back door squeaks open, and seconds later I hear the vet's truck roar out the lane. Kate comes into the kitchen and shakes her finger at Chase.

"You know I don't like you sitting on the table, Chase. We have chairs."

"Oops. I forgot," Chase says, giving her a cheeky grin. She just rolls her eyes at him.

The room falls silent. Chase gives me a look and jerks his head Kate's way. So, are you going to tell her? his eyes ask.

As exciting as this news is, I'm starting to second guess picking up that phone. Is Kate going to be mad that I took her phone call? I still have a scar on my upper arm from Mrs. McLeod digging her fingernails into my skin after I grabbed the landline. No one was around, and I was just trying to be helpful. I thought Mrs. McLeod would love me if I only did enough. I was so naive at seven years old. It's better to run away from love, because you sure can't earn it.

Oh well. Maybe Kate should get mad at me before I let my guard down any farther. It's better if it happens now, because she's slowly but surely wearing me down. The walls around my heart are starting to crumble, and it's scaring me.

Kate and Chase are both staring at me now, Chase with an encouraging look in his eyes, and Kate with a confused expression on her face.

"Um, your phone rang while you were outside, and…" Okay, I need to get my voice under control here. You don't care, Taz. You don't belong here, and you don't want to belong here. You got this.

I straighten my shoulders and look Kate dead in the eyes.

"Anyway, I answered it for you, and they told me Moriah got moved, and I'm getting a new social worker."

"I came in here, and she was dancing around like a kangaroo on Red Bull," Chase adds with a fake southern drawl. "I didn't know what hit her at first, but then she came to."

I glare at him, so he knows his comments are *not* welcome, before turning my back and facing Kate.

She smiles. "Well, that is good news. That woman…" her voice trails off. "Do you know if they've appointed a new one yet?"

"Yeah, it's some Bailey Rand. She's coming sometime within the next week," I supply.

"Well, let's hope Miss Rand is better. Now, does anyone want a glass of chocolate milk? And Chase, how's the chicken?"

Chase opens his mouth to give the latest updates when the back door closes with a bang. Rainey comes racing in, her blonde hair flying behind her in a wild curtain and a black chicken in her arms.

"Chase! Chase!" She pants. "Thelma pecked her bandage off!" She shoves the squirming bird into Chase's arms.

"I brought another stick and some duct tape this time. Maybe that will work." She pulls a popsicle stick out of her back pocket and slides the rolls of duct tape off her upper arm. The chicken gives a loud squawk as its injured leg dangles loosely against Chase's forearm.

Rainey is bent over, trying to catch her breath, so Chase thrusts the chicken in my direction.

"Uh-uh. I am not holding that creature. It stinks worse than the goats," I protest, taking a step back.

"Well, I can't splint it and hold it," Chase argues, continuing to offer me the chicken. I glance over at Kate. She's busy pouring milk into cups, fighting to keep a straight face. She catches my eye and mouths, "All you, kid."

I groan and hold my hands out. "How do you hold a chicken, anyway?"

"Here." Chase guides my hands into the right position around the chicken. The creature protests loudly and flaps its wings. I drop it and jump back, and the bird attempts to hop away one-footed. It doesn't get very far before it collapses in a heap.

"You killed my bird!" Rainey accuses, no longer out of breath.

"It attacked me!" I shoot back before surveying the lump of feathers. Thelma is most certainly not dead. If anything, her fall has made her louder.

Chase picks up the injured bird and patiently shows me how to hold it again. This time, I squeeze it tight to my chest. I despise this thing even more than the goats, and that's saying something, but Rainey doesn't need to see death up this close.

"Whoa, don't crush it," Chase laughs as the chicken makes a gurgling sound. I loosen my hold by a fraction and watch him break the stick down to the right size.

He leans over the chicken, and his sun-browned hands are gentle as he sets Thelma's leg against the popsicle stick and tapes it up.

"Okay, now we need to add something to keep her from pecking it. Duck tape is strong, but I don't think it will be enough." He straightens up, and his grey eyes meet mine for a second. I look away. Something about this guy is making my heart race right now, and I don't like it.

"What if we turned the duct tape inside out?" Rainey suggests, stroking Thelma's ebony back. "Then if she tried to peck it, her beak would stick, and she'd learn her lesson."

"I don't think that would quite work, Rainey," Chase answers, looking down at her. "I don't think the stickiness would be enough to deter Thelma.

"Is there a flavour that chickens hate?" I blurt out, an idea starting to form. "You could rub it on the tape to keep her from pulling it off."

Chase's face lights up. "Hey, that's a good idea! But I have no idea what they hate. Those birds will eat a lot of stuff."

"Currently googling it," Kate calls from the counter.

"They eat bugs and worms," Rainey says, wrinkling her nose up in disgust. "That's really, really gross."

I laugh. "Bugs aren't so bad. Do you know what is gross, though?"

"What?" Rainey asks eagerly.

"Squishy mushrooms with grape jam," I tell her. Mrs. Baker's kids used to devour them for snack, and I was forced to either eat it with them or go hungry until supper.

"Ew!" Rainey pretends to barf. "No one eats that, though. You made it up."

"No, I didn't. I promise," I insist.

"We can try cinnamon," Kate calls from the kitchen counter. "Or garlic, or paprika."

She rummages through her spice drawer. Thelma is getting a little heavy in my arms, and I'm starting to have visions of her laying an egg on me when something wet and squishy runs down my hand. I hastily let Thelma go, and she drops to the floor with a thud.

"Hey! Don't drop my chicken! That's not nice!" Rainey yells, putting her hands on her hips.

"The stupid thing pooped on me!" I retort, eyeing the white mess all over my hand. "This is disgusting!"

"That's not just poop," Rainey informs me as she follows me to the bathroom. "The white part is actually chicken pee, and the sprinkles in it are the poop."

"I don't care what it is," I mutter. "Either way, it's gross."

"Well, I don't feel sorry for you, because you dropped Thelma twice, and you called her stupid. Thelma's not stupid," Rainey announces as she watches me scrub the manure off my hand.

"I had a valid reason to drop your chicken both times," I argue.

"I'd hold onto Thelma even if she tried to bite me to death," Rainey says, crossing her arms over her chest. "I love Thelma."

"Well, it's good someone does," I mutter under my breath. I almost say something about chicken nuggets, but decide I'd better not traumatize the little girl further. I congratulate myself on my self control as I follow Rainey back to the kitchen.

Kate is holding the chicken while Chase wraps more duct tape around the splint, this time with the sticky side out. Then Kate takes the bird to the kitchen sink and holds it over while Chase shakes some orange powder onto the leg. I bite my lip to avoid saying more jokes about seasoned chicken tenders as Rainey goes over and pats Thelma's head.

"Okay, hopefully that will do the trick," Chase announces, closing the bottle of paprika and tossing it on the counter. Kate hands the chicken to Rainey.

"Be careful not to get the paprika on your clothes, or it might stain," Kate cautions.

"These are barn clothes. It doesn't matter." Rainey gives Kate a 'duh' look and hugs her bird close. The dumb thing snuggles down into her arms. Why couldn't it have behaved like that for me?

Chase runs a hand through his hair, making it stick up on end, and grins at his little sister.

"You'd better give Thelma some extra corn tonight after all she's been through," he says.

Rainey nods solemnly. "I will. I'll give her two scoops instead of one."

"Are you going to wait and walk home with Parker and me?" he wonders next.

Rainey shakes her head. "No, I'll take Thelma home so she can rest."

"Imagine having that much love for a chicken," I mutter to myself after she's gone. Chase laughs and starts swinging up on the table before Kate stops him with a look.

"Yeah, she's quite the kid," he agrees, plopping down into a chair. "But I wouldn't trade her for the world."

I turn away to hide a grin. These people aren't so bad. If only I could trust them enough to get close; close enough to share my hopes and dreams and fears. But it'll be a frosty day in July before that happens.

A door slams shut from somewhere above us, and soon Parker and Madame Lemair appear on the stairs. Parker smiles shyly at me, and I wave to him. He comes over and stands right in front of me, tipping his head back. His brown eyes find mine, and he whispers, "Do you want to see what I painted today?"

"I'd love to see what you painted today," I answer honestly.

Parker surprises me by slipping his hand in mine and leading me toward the stairs. I look back as we head for the second floor and see Madame and Kate talking in low voices. Madame is smiling softly, and Kate has this proud look on her face as she watches us go.

We go past the family portrait in the hall, past my room with AJ's letter still lying out on the desk and stop at the foot of the attic stairs. Parker lets go of my hand and says, "You go first. The stairs are kind of steep, so then I can catch you if you fall."

I open my mouth to protest. Parker could never stop a falling Taz. But then I shut my mouth and start up the narrow flight of steps. This isn't about falling down the stairs- it's bigger than that. I have a feeling Parker doesn't often offer to catch people.

Parker's latest painting is still drying on the big wooden easel. The top half of it is bleak and cold. A couple scrawny birds peck the dead, brittle grass in vain, and the bare ground stands out starkly against the gray sky. A few wispy clouds bravely chase each other across the frigid expanse, while a wrought iron bench sits empty beneath, as though no human life is willing to brave the cold.

But beneath the frozen crust, the earth teems with life. The dirt changes to a rich, warm brown. Earthworms wriggle happily toward the surface, and colourful seeds are sending shoots up from deep underground. The bare beginnings of an oak tree are splitting their way through the protective shell of an acorn, and a small gopher stretches sleepily in its burrow. Brilliant green beetles are also heading for the top, clearing tiny trails as they go. On the surface, a caterpillar stretches beneath a rock, and a red and black snake flicks its tongue out of its nest, as if testing the air to see if winter is over.

"I call this one 'Hope'," Parker says. I can see him watching me out of the corner of my eye as I reach a finger out to the painting. I pause a centimeter above the gopher. The fur looks so real that I want to touch it. That's when I notice three words woven into the dirt near the bottom of the scene. *Spring will come*.

"That's amazing," I breathe. "This one's a winner for sure."

Parker doesn't smile, exactly, but his face gets this pleased look on it, and he stands a little taller.

"How long did this take you?" I ask.

"Thirteen hours and forty-two minutes," he responds immediately.

I shouldn't be surprised that he keeps track of the time right down to the minute. It's such a Parker thing.

The phrase on the painting keeps running around my head as I follow Parker back down the stairs.

Spring has come and almost gone in Iowa, but my life still feels like winter. Does hope ever skip people?

CHAPTER 13

"adame Lemair is very impressed with you, Taz," Kate says, setting down her coffee cup.

I pick a cranberry off the top of my muffin and shrug. "I haven't done anything special. Parker just likes me for some reason."

"Madame said you're a natural at picking up on his emotions and acting accordingly. She's never seen him hold anyone's hand voluntarily before yesterday, and she's noticed he looks you in the eyes a lot more than with most people."

I keep picking at my muffin, a little embarrassed. He's a cool kid, and I like his paintings, but I'm no child psych expert.

Kate takes a slurp of coffee before continuing, "Parker's mom also said he talks about you sometimes. She asked him how painting was yesterday, and he got this little smile on his face and said, 'Taz liked it.'"

"Cool," I finally mumble. I don't have a great track record on dealing with myself. Parker could pick a hundred better role models than me.

"Anyway, you'd better get ready. I can run you over to Chloe's in half an hour." Kate picks up her empty cup and takes it over to the sink. I sigh and wonder if this day will ever end. Goat chores this morning took forever. There's a bummer kid that needs to be bottle fed because the nanny is sick, and the thing was so uncooperative this morning. At least tonight is the last of my 'punishment' chores. Now I get to spend my extra hours studying for exams in two weeks instead. Breakfast was long and drawn out, too, and I hope swimming at Chloe's makes the day go faster. I have places to be tonight.

We went shopping the other day after school for a swimsuit, and I'm rummaging around in the catch-all drawer in the kitchen for scissors to cut the tags off when I spy a flashlight and remember AJ's letter, now lying forgotten on my dresser. I grab it and the scissors and head back upstairs, shutting the door behind me.

I cut the tags and throw my suit and a towel into a bag before turning my attention to the letter. I smooth it out on my dresser and shine the flashlight onto the missing words. Nothing jumps out, so I pick the paper up and shine the flashlight in from the back. I squint my eyes at the black scrawl.

"Okay, that says guard…and that's rolt, no riot…okay, and that's…oh, that's the name of the hospital."

Piecing the letter together is harder than I thought it would be, but eventually I figure it out. There was a riot, and later some guy got hurt by a guard and had to go to the hospital in some town that starts with an *S*.

I crumple the letter up in a ball and throw it against the wall. It bounces off and rolls under the bed. Juvie is getting worse and worse for AJ. And what am I doing- going to a pool party?

I've heard of people getting survivor's guilt from escaping a car crash unharmed when others didn't, but I'm beginning to wonder if survivor's guilt is also possible when someone gets a harsher sentence than you. Because that's what I'm feeling right now.

Kate knocks on my door, and I grab my bag from where it landed in a corner and follow her out to the truck.

At least I can write him letters to keep his spirits high, I tell myself as the truck rolls out the lane. He said he likes those.

The trip to Chloe's farm is a short one. We turn into the lane on the other side of Chase's and drive by acres of rolling wheat up to a massive, modern stone house. The lane continues past the house and opens into a giant gravel yard. Huge machinery sheds line three sides of it, and an enormous green tractor with tracks is sitting out in front, hitched to a massive cultivator. I may not be a farm kid, but I've been in Iowa long enough to know this operation is big, even for around here.

Kate pulls into the driveway in front of the house, and we get out. I'm almost afraid to set foot on the polished white walkway, but Kate marches up to the front door in her dirty sneakers like she's done this a thousand times before. I should have known Chloe's rich if she has an in-ground pool in her backyard, but I wasn't expecting this.

Kate raps on the door, and I wait for a butler in a dark vest to open it. Instead, we're greeted by a middle-aged woman, dressed in the most ordinary sweatpants and T-shirt. A golden-haired toddler is clinging to her leg, and two girls are fighting over something in the background.

"Come on in," Mrs. Davidson invites with a smile. She pushes back a strand of brilliant orange hair, unfazed by the fact that two of her children are throwing flour all over her spotless kitchen.

Chloe comes sliding down the banister, another boy right behind her. They slip off the railing and land in a heap on the floor at our feet. Chloe laughs and helps her brother to his feet.

"Get off my foot, Simon! Oh hi, Taz." She grins, her wild hair frizzing up like a halo around her face.

"Mom!" a shrill voice interrupts us from the kitchen table. "Mom, Chelsea got flour in my hair!"

I catch a glimpse of the younger girl dumping a cupful of flour onto the other girl's head, turning the yelling into sputtering. Mrs. Davidson sighs and heads for the kitchen table, but Simon beats her there, and it soon turns into a free-for-all blizzard of flying flour. Chloe grabs my arm and pulls me upstairs, away from the mess, and Kate waves at me before letting herself out the door.

Chloe's room is at the top of the twisting marble staircase, and we both collapse on the bed.

"Are those kids all yours?" I joke.

Chloe laughs. "Yup. And there's two more outside somewhere with Chad Dad."

I know its impolite to let your eyes bug out, but that's what mine are doing right now. "You have seven kids?" And I thought the Bakers had their hands full with five.

"Well, not me personally," Chloe retorts. "But Chad Dad and Mom do."

"Cha-what?" I quirk an eyebrow at her.

Chloe rolls onto her stomach, giggling. "Chad Dad. His name's Chad, and he's my dad, so… anyway, do you want to go swimming?"

"You're a poet, and you don't know it," I mumble under my breath as I grab my bag and follow Chloe. We scamper to the other side of the house and take a much narrower flight of stairs down into the laundry room. We dodge toy trucks and leap over piles of dirty laundry to get to the other side. Chloe stops abruptly outside the room, and I fall into her.

"Whoa. Pool's out here," she says, catching me and ushering the way out onto the back deck.

The toddler has made it out here by now, and he's driving a toy dump truck around the outdoor kitchen. Chloe jumps over his head while I walk around him up the short flight of steps to the pool gate.

"Make sure you shut it tight behind you whenever you go in or out," Chloe cautions, holding it open for me like a chauffeur. "I rather like my six siblings, and I don't want any of them to drown."

"Dark way to put it, but fair enough," I nod. We walk past a row of white lounge chairs overlooking the sparkling kidney bean shaped pool. A rock waterfall churns up bubbles along the far end. A water slide is skillfully built into the stones without ruining the aesthetic, and a small white diving board juts out nearby. A marble hot tub bubbles merrily in the far corner, with a white plastic kiddie pool beside. The whole setup looks like it costs more than the Bakers' whole house did.

Chloe walks right by it all like it's nothing, which I guess it isn't to her, and leads the way to a large hut with an outdoor shower in front.

The hut is cool and dark, and curtained off into three separate change rooms. I shrug into my swimsuit and run for the water.

I dive in, and the cool water ripples around me. Foster parents number three, or maybe it was four, made me take lessons at the YMCA one summer, and it's a skill I've never regretted having. There's something about water that washes everything else away- all the fear and discouragement and abandonment.

I break the surface and get splashed by Chloe's cannonball. I splutter and wipe the spray out of my eyes. She pops up and grins.

"Sorry," she yells, diving away as I attempt to get her back. We chase each other around the deep end until we're both so out of breath, we grip the edge of the pool to stay afloat.

Chloe recovers in about two seconds and jumps out for a run down the slide while I'm still wondering if my lungs will ever work again. She whizzes down and hits the water with a splash. I take my chance and move in while she's still under the surface and greet her with a wave in the face as she comes up for air.

"Gotcha!" I yell, and swim as fast as I can for the ledge.

I'm almost out of the water when a hand grabs my ankle, and she pulls me back in. Water gets up my nose as I go under, and I can feel my sinuses burning. I kick for the surface and come up, choking on the chlorinated liquid.

"Are you okay?" Chloe asks with a laugh. I don't answer and let myself slide back under the surface. I open my eyes a crack and watch her leg churn up the water as she heads over to see if I'm okay. Closer, closer, and…I push myself out if the water with a big splash, and the chase begins all over again.

Finally, we haul ourselves out of the water, thoroughly exhausted. I drag my weary muscles over to one of the lounge chairs. Chloe picks up a little handheld radio from a basket near one of the chairs and calls for someone to bring us drinks and snacks.

Chloe leans back in her chair and gives me a sideways glance. "Just so you know, when the staff brings the snacks, you're not supposed to offer to help her set them down or anything. It's highly offensive."

I open my mouth to ask about any more of this staff etiquette, then snap it shut again when I see the twinkle in her eyes.

"Trust me, I know all about staff," I reassure her. "The last place I stayed in ran like a British manor."

"Right," Chloe snickers. She sits up and shades her eyes with an arm so she can see me through the sunlight. "I bet you have been to a lot of cool places, though."

Her questioning gaze is open and friendly, but inside, I can feel the doors closing around my heart. Wrong question, friend.

I try to go for the light-hearted approach and nod. "Oh, for sure. I've stayed at farms, ranches, city houses, even an old schoolhouse. Fifteen states and counting. I've been all over." Half of that isn't true, but she doesn't need to know that.

She gives me another curious look. To my relief, Mrs. Davidson comes to the rescue by setting a tray of tall, frosted drinks and fruit down on the low table between our chairs. One of the girls, the older one from the flour fight, follows her with a basket of salty snacks.

We dive into the snacks, but the food doesn't stop Chloe from wanting to talk.

"So, how are you liking Oakville so far?" she asks around a mouthful of chips.

I shrug. "It's small." What else is there to say? The only good things here are the races and Talia…and Chase, if I'm honest with myself.

Chloe giggles. "You got that right. But small-town vibes are the best. Wait until the Fourth of July, and the Harvest Festival, and the Five Churches Potluck, and…"

I let her ramble on about the amazing qualities of her town; at least, it keeps her from asking me personal questions. I already know she'll never convince me this town is so great. I do notice that the dirt bike races aren't even an honourable mention on her Top Ten List of Oakville's Wonderful Things to Do.

I manage to keep the conversation away from anything too deep for the next few hours as we lounge around in the sun, try out her oldest brother's gaming setup, and take one of their four ATVs for a spin. It's fun, but I breath a sigh of relief when I see Kate's Chevy rolling in the lane.

Mrs. Davidson gives me a hug that smells like homemade cookies before I leave, and Chloe and her siblings line up on the driveway and wave as we go out the lane.

"So, how was it?" Kate asks as soon as our tires hit the blacktop.

I know what she's thinking- apart from Chase, she doesn't know what friends I have. When she caught me sneaking in and I said I was with 'friends', I told her it was kids from church, and I didn't want to reveal their names. I know she didn't buy that one, so I have a feeling she's relieved I have at least one good 'church friend' to hang out with.

So, I tell her "It was great," and paste a big smile on my face. I tried to have fun and be nice. I owe it to Chloe after snubbing her repeated attempts at a closer friendship. Inside, however, I know

I'm not going back to her house. She's alright from a distance, but her type, the kind that like to 'talk', are too dangerous. Talia's more my style.

CHAPTER 14

Kate is taking forever to get to bed tonight. After a leisurely bath, she bumps around in her room until ten thirty, before turning on her lamp and reading for another half hour. I stand outside her door, tearing out my hair waiting for her light to click off. I'm going to be late.

It's half past eleven when Kate's gentle breathing turns into a light snore. I tiptoe past her door and down the stairs to the garage. I slip into my sneakers and grab a light sweater to ward off the night's chill before softly closing the door behind me. I inch around to the side of the house and grab my bike before heading off into the night.

The address Talia gave me for our meeting place is in an old section of town, out beyond the grain elevator and the Co-op. The police have been hanging around the school more since the bust at the brick factory, so we've had to improvise.

Our new meeting place is a crumbling brick apartment building with chipped paint and rusted metal railings. A dark figure rises from the front steps and hurries toward me as I edge out of the shadows. Talia raises a hand in greeting.

"You're late," she comments as she leads me behind the apartment complex.

"Sorry. Kate wouldn't fall asleep," I apologize.

Talia smiles faintly as she pulls a rusted black bike out of the weeds. "Must be a nice problem to have."

I open my mouth to protest, but the wistfulness in her voice stops me. "I guess so," I finally mumble.

"This is my place, by the way," she grunts, jerking a thumb in the direction of the dirty building. "My brother and I have lived here for a few years. It's fine as long as Mom stays away with one of her boyfriends. She always comes crawling back home eventually, though. Unfortunately."

I just nod, because there's nothing else to say or do. Sometimes the people in your life get so messed up it's better when they leave.

The streetlights fade in the distance, and the thick darkness descends on us like a blanket. The only sound is the whizzing of our bike tires on the blacktop. I flick the single light on at the front of my bike and follow close behind Talia as she turns onto a tiny dirt pass. My light bounces off a gleaming yellow 'No Winter Maintenance' sign before we disappear back into the night.

The great, hulking shadows of tractors and machinery are the only disruption in the dark, rippling sea of fields. Talia tells me to go ahead with my light, so we don't fall off the edge of the road and into the ditch. A person could disappear without much trouble among the gently rolling hills and scattered clumps of trees. Out on this lonely road, it's tempting to ride on forever and never come back.

"Turn up here," Talia's command breaks the eerie stillness.

I squint through the darkness and slow down, searching for the turnoff. A larger dirt road intersects with the cow path we're on, and I make a sharp left turn.

"There's a paved road about half a mile up ahead," Talia says, coming up beside me. "Misty Lane. That'll lead us right into Staten."

My legs are starting to burn from the constant pedaling, and Talia's breathing is getting stronger and harsher. The turnoff to Misty Lane feels light-years away.

"We're almost there." Talia gasps as we're met with yet another hill.

"We can do it," I pant back, leaning on my handlebars. My legs feel like jelly by the time we crest the top of the hill, but the thin thread of blacktop winding off to the left renews our energy. Soon we're pedaling as fast as we can down the smooth surface of the road into Staten.

"Car," Talia yells, as a set of headlights break through the night, and we both dive into the ditch, bikes and all. I tilt my head up and look at the stars, trying to ignore the handlebar stabbing into my side, as we wait for the vehicle to pass.

What am I doing here? The thought flashes across my wind like a lightning bolt. It's not 'what am I doing in Staten'; it's 'what am I doing here, alive, on earth'? What stroke of fate, or if you're like the rest of Oakville, God, decided to put a kid like me, with no place to belong, on this earth? Do I have a purpose?

The car passes us by long before I come up with an answer, and I shrug the uncomfortable questions out of my mind.

This is what happens when you slow down, I tell myself. I push my body to the max and soar past Talia down the road. The wind whistles past me, and I'm free. I could go on forever. Maybe by the time I ran out of road, I'd have answers.

"Wait up, girl!" she calls after me. I brake to a stop and wait for her to catch up.

"What got into you? You were flying!" she says, tilting her head to one side with a curious look. "I thought that bike was gonna fall apart on you."

I shrug my shoulders and give her a lopsided grin for an answer. "How close are we?" I ask, changing the subject.

Talia squints at the nearest mailbox. "That's 1478, and we want 1510, so we're close."

We slow pedal down the road, searching the edge of the ditch for more mailboxes. The handful of houses scattered in a wiggly line are old and rundown, with crusted siding and rusty trucks in the driveways. Most are only illuminated by a single, dirty bulb, hanging by a thread over the front doors.

"Here it is," Talia whispers, skidding to a stop beside a dented mailbox at the end of a long, winding lane. A thick stand of hickory trees hides the house, but streaks of light manage to work their way through the leaves. Someone is home.

We ditch our bikes behind a sturdy oak across the road, and creep into the thicket. The lower branches slap my face, so I drop to my hands and knees. Talia follows suit behind me as I feel my way through the undergrowth. A dead twig snaps beneath my hand, and we freeze. The only sound that answers is our quiet breathing, so we keep going.

The thicket thins out, and I drop to my stomach and slither right up to the edge of the yard. I stop once the grass tickles my face. Talia slides up beside me.

Her house is an old blue trailer with a sagging wooden deck and a small fire pit out front. A string of lights illuminates an empty flowerbed and a narrow strip of green lawn before the yard turns to dirt. The house windows are dark, but the small, cinder block shop off to one side is blazing with light.

Through the open overhead door, we can see a slight, dark-haired woman bent over a bike. Tools are strewn in a pile around here, but the rest of the floor is neat and clean.

"Can we get closer?" Talia whispers, her breath tickling my ear.

"I doubt it," I murmur back. "The shop lights will give us away as soon as we get out of the trees."

I rest my chin on the backs of my hands and watch the girl. She seems to know exactly what she's doing. I wish I was brave enough to go talk to her. I'd ask her why she's fixing her bike at one in the morning, how she got so good at dirt biking, and where she works. What's her real name, her dreams, her hobbies?

Who is she as a person?

We sit there for another half hour or so before deciding that nothing exciting is going to happen. We slither back through the trees and grab our bikes before starting the long ride back home.

"Well…now we know where she lives," Talia says, sounding very underwhelmed. "But we still don't know who she is or where she came from or why. Is dirt biking her only source of income, or does she just enjoy showing the other riders up, or what's her deal?" She pounds her handlebars in frustration. "Even the mailbox didn't hold a clue. It said 'Geiger' on the side, and I'm not convinced that's her real name."

"It was worth it, though," I decide, legs screaming as I bike up another hill. "We saw her- the real her, not the leave-everyone-in-the-dust-biker her. We know she doesn't have another vehicle, probably lives alone, and takes better care of her house than most people in Staten."

"Fair enough," Talia admits grudgingly. "I guess we did learn a bit."

We bike the rest of the way back in silence, and part ways outside of town. I keep a wary eye out for young cops with green eyes sitting on side roads, but the ride home is uneventful.

I park my bike beside the garage and tiptoe inside. I glance at the clock in the living room as I go by and groan inwardly. Church tomorrow is going to be fun on three hours of sleep.

* * *

I rub my tired eyes as I tiptoe to the office. Kate is taking her Sunday afternoon nap, and I should take one, too, but I haven't checked my email in too long.

I pause in front of the large family portrait on the wall. Kate's dad smiles faintly back at me. I wish he was still alive so I could talk to him. How did he get from a car crash at the corner of

Dubuque to a mansion on a hill with a lovely wife and two cute kids? I guess I could talk to the pastor instead, but I'm not in the habit of asking men of cloth anything about life.

I trace my finger over the young boy's face. Who is he? He must live somewhere far away, because the only communication Kate has with him are long phone calls, usually when she thinks I'm not around. Maybe he's her anchor, keeping her sane while she tries to take care of a crazy delinquent like me.

I move over to Kate's mom. I heard somewhere that she moved to Louisiana soon after her husband's death to help her older sister, who is dying of cancer. She looks like a sweet woman, but there's fire behind her gentle gaze. She seems like the kind of person who isn't afraid to walk into the middle of a hurricane if need be.

I sigh and move on down the hall to the office. I log into my email and open the only new message in my inbox. It's from Micah.

> to: taz4ever
> from: micdawson
> subject: re: the bro
>
> got more info on aj the center he's at is pretty tight rite now. theres been sum fights there. have been able to talk to him though and he says to not worry about jack rite now things are settling down a bit. who is jack though?
> if one of the riots blows up though maybe we can manage to make him disappear, but it would be sketchy because almost every juvenile escapee gets caught and that just makes things worse. hes kind of in rough shape right now cause his nose got busted up in another fight but he will be

okay cause he's tough
M

I sit back in my chair and loop my fingers together behind my head and bite my lip. If Micah could get AJ out of there, that would both amazing and terrifying. Escape is freedom, but capture puts you worse off than before, and 9.9 times out of 10, it's the latter that happens.

CHAPTER 15

"For your final project this year, I want you to do a piece titled 'Life'. You may use any medium you want; my goal is for you to use your creativity to express what comes to your mind when you think of life."

The chalk squeaks across the blackboard as Mrs. Woodrow writes down the four-letter word. I lean back in my chair and sigh.

"Why does she always make us do such deep themes?" I complain to Ivan. He shrugs his bony shoulders and gives me a bewildered look. To him, life is no more than a fantasy, filled with flying horses and fire-breathing dragons. I didn't expect him to have the answer, anyway.

One of Chloe's friends, Shelby or Shelley or whatever her name is, raises her hand from the back. "How do we know if we're doing it right if that's all we have for an outline?" she whines.

Mrs. Woodrow smiles patiently. "There are no wrong answers; it's simply your perception of what 'life' means."

Well, what if I don't have perception? I twirl my pencil around and around between my fingers and study the blank paper on my desk. Ivan is already off to the races, sketching out a swirling vortex. I sigh and wonder if a blank paper has ever given anyone answers before. I could do something generic, like a tiny seedling or a newborn baby. Those things are life. I wonder what Talia's doing; I bet she's having the same problem as I am. Chase is most likely sketching out a cross or another goat.

I get up and wander to the paint cabinet to see if one of the colourful jars will strike inspiration within me. I can think of a lot of things that aren't life, like drugs and iron bars and green-eyed policemen and moms who leave.

"What are you gonna do?" Talia asks, coming up behind me.

I shrug and run my fingers over the jars of paint. "I have no clue. How does she expect a couple ninth graders to know what the meaning of 'life' is? I feel like that's something even philosophers struggle with."

"I'm gonna do a baby animal, like a duck," Talia decides, grabbing the container of 'sunset yellow'.

I sigh and grab a jar of 'leaf green'. Why am I making such a big deal out of this, anyway? I'll paint a seedling and be done with it. Mrs. Woodrow must be tired of me handing in artwork full of plants, but she's going to have to deal with it.

I slide back into my seat and prop up my tabletop easel. I toss the blank paper aside- who needs to make a sketch for a plant? Beside me, Ivan is mixing deep shades of purples, blues, and grays together on his palette. A wide swirl of black is already on his canvas.

I dip my brush into a small pot of deep brown paint and make a wide swath across the bottom of my page. I mix in some deeper browns, grays, and blacks to make a rough mound of dirt. Soon it reminds me of a less realistic version of Parker's painting, 'Hope', except there's no life brimming in mine- yet.

I tilt my head and eye the canvas, trying to picture a thin little seedling on top of the earth.

"What if I'd add the seed beneath the surface, too?" I muse to myself. "That might look better."

While I wait for the bottom layer to dry, I wander around the room. Chloe's friend is painting a baby holding a small puppy in its hands, with a row of flowers coming up in the background. I guess she wanted to make sure she covered her bases and put as many newborn things in there as she could. She's one of those kids that wants to get a scholarship to college, not because she needs the funds, but to prove she can. Her seatmate is painting a watercolour silhouette of a woman sitting on a dock. The model's face is turned toward the sea, gazing at the sunset. The sinking ball of fire makes me wonder if she's trying to portray the end of life, instead of the beginning like everyone else.

Talia is outlining a cartoon duck in a kiddie pool, while beside her Chase is deep into a picture of a stormy sea. I didn't think he's had that bad of a life, but those waves he's making look huge.

I meander back to my seat and touch the tip of a finger to my painting. It's dry, so I pick up the 'leaf green' and start outlining the frail stem of a new plant. The stalk reaches out for the sky, its little baby leaves starting to unfurl. It looks so vulnerable; a storm or a boot is all it would take to crush the seedling forever. It's like me.

A part of me is starting to wonder if I might stay in Oakville. Kate has had a lot of chances to get rid of me, but she hasn't. I'm making friends, settling into school, even listening better in church. And I'm terrified; terrified that someone will crush the tiny light of hope inside, terrified a storm will blow it out, terrified my life will continue on the path to destruction, and there's nothing I can do to stop it.

I trace the stem down below the surface before pausing to mix a few different browns together. The resulting champagne colour is perfect for the tiny seed that gives life to the plant. I twirl a few spidery roots down deep into the dirt from the bottom of the seed. The seed is safe, safe from the storm and wind and crushing footsteps. But it never gets to see the sun. Which is better, darkness behind walls of safety, or the flickering, fragile light of hope?

I sigh and sit back to survey my painting. It's not a masterpiece, but it'll do. One glance at my seatmate's painting confirms that.

Ivan's painting is a deep, dark hole that spins outward in a dizzying array of light and shadows before fading off the edges of the canvas. He's busy painting words in a looping scroll, coming out of the black center. I lean closer and squint my eyes to see better.

"Life is but a vapor…okay then. You do you," I shrug, turning back to my own space. Why do some people have to paint such weird things?

Ivan grins and scratches his chin, leaving behind a smear of cobalt blue. "Life is like a feather that vanishes in the wind. It's like a beam of light, quickly disappearing into the vortex. Life is nothing, yet life is everything."

"Okay, okay, I get the point," I say, throwing my hands up. I don't get it, but the last thing I need is some teen philosopher telling me what life is all about.

I take my jars of paint back to the cupboard and take my brushes to the double sink. Chase comes up behind me and dumps his stuff into the adjoining basin with a loud crash before turning on the tap.

"What did you paint?" he asks curiously as he waits for his sink to fill with hot water.

I submerge my brush under water and shrug. "Just a little plant. Nothing special," I mutter, focusing on digging the dried paint out of the bristles. I have a funny feeling that this conversation could get deep quickly, and I don't do deep conversations, especially with guys like Chase.

"Did you see Ivan's painting?" I ask, steering the conversation away from my artwork.

He laughs and nods his head. "Yeah, that one's different." He pauses and scrubs at a brush handle. "He's got a point, though. Life *is* pretty short."

Why does Chase always have to see the good in every situation?

This is taking, for lack of a better word, a deep turn.

"Are you almost done there, Taz?" Chloe's friend asks sweetly, squeezing in between me and Chase. Like half the other girls in my grade, she's sweet on Chase, and would love to be washing brushes beside him.

I slow down my scrubbing a tad and try to sound sorry. "I've still got a few things left, Shelly."

"It's Shelby," she retorts.

Oops. Shelby sounds a little uptight. Could there be a hint of jealousy in the air?

"If it's only a few, I can quick wash them for you," Shelby says, a little anxiously. "I want to get my stuff washed before the bell rings.

Right, because the bell is going to ring in a whole half hour. That's not nearly enough time to wash a handful of brushes and a paint palette, I think. But if she's offering…

"Go for it, " I say, stepping back from the sink. I don't even feel bad that my grossest brush still needs to be washed; she kind of brought this on herself. I'm not going to fight her to stand beside some guy. Chase might be nice, but I need to stay away from him. As much as I wish I could get attached, it's too risky. Oakville is growing on me; I just wish I could see the future and know if this is where I'll stay. This thing called 'life' usually throws a nasty curve ball right in my face as soon as I let down my guard.

Mrs. Woodrow stops me as I take my easel over to the counter by the windows to dry. She makes that 'uhm-hmm' noise that teachers seem to love as she surveys the piece with a critical eye. I shift from foot to foot and chew the inside of my lip, waiting for her to move on.

With a final stroke of her chin, she nods once and looks at me. "Very interesting, Taz. What inspired this picture?"

"Um," I stutter, trying to buy time. I don't think 'because

it was easy' will cut it. C'mon, Taz, you're the kid who can get yourself out of anything.

"Well," I finally continue, "I guess a plant reminds me of life because…because it grows, and…" Okay, this is getting off to a bad start. I mentally scratch my head for a better answer. "And I guess a plant needs water and sun to grow, like we need things to grow, and the growing seeds remind me of life, I guess." There's no way I'm sharing my true thoughts with her.

My sentences are going in circles, and they don't make sense even to me, but hopefully Mrs. Woodrow will be too confused to ask more questions. She wrinkles her nose and opens her mouth, then shuts it and nods politely, before letting me go put my painting on the counter. I gently set my easel down before taking a step back to survey the other finished canvases.

Chase's artwork is sitting by itself at the very end of the row. The stormy sea whips around a rocky island in the center of the image. A tall, striped lighthouse rises in a solid line from the middle, weathering the waves like a fortress. A brilliant yellow beacon shines from the top of the tower, reaching feeble fingers into the night.

Chase steps up beside me and leans on the counter as I'm examining the picture. I'm not sure how he managed to escape Shelby's clutches, and I'm not about to ask.

"This is cool. Painting must run in the family," I tell him, pointing to the lighthouse.

He laughs and shakes his head, making his hair flop from side to side. "Nah, Parker's got a leg up on me in that category. I did get the idea from one of his paintings, though. Maybe you've seen it already- the one of a sailboat in a storm?"

"Resilience," I respond with a nod.

"Resilience?" Chase gives me a funny look.

"That's what he called the painting," I say. I can't believe Chase doesn't know the title. That's one of the most important parts of Parker's paintings.

"Sure. Anyway, I guess you could say that's what inspired me. No one's life is perfect. We've all got waves and rainy days, but we must choose to build a lighthouse on the rocks and shine through it, or we'll drown."

For once, one of Chase's big ideas makes perfect sense. After he wanders off, I look at a few more paintings, but they're all a piddly description of life compared to that strong, striped fortress.

I notice another thing about Chase's painting- the lighthouse is a solitary figure, yet its light keeps burning. My mantra has always been that most storms are best weathered alone. Is there a way to keep a spark of hope aflame without breaking the walls that protect me?

CHAPTER 16

"Are you excited for the last week of school?" Kate asks, sitting down across from me and my science textbook at the kitchen table.

I turn the page and groan at yet another diagram, this one a depiction of the human skeleton. Who knew there were so many bones in one body?

"I will be after I get this stupid exam out of the way," I mumble, studying the graphic. "At least I don't have to do the full book exam like everyone else."

Because the science program at my school back in Ottumwa was different, my science teacher here made an exam for me on the units I've actually studied this semester. Otherwise, I would have had to cram three new units before into the last month of school. I am forever grateful to him for his generosity, especially when I look through the seven-page study guide he made.

Kate takes a slurp of her go-to morning beverage and nods. "That was nice of him to remake a copy of the exam to suit what you've learned. I always did like Mr. Galloway as a teacher."

I grunt in response. I'm not feeling very talkative right now, considering that my new social worker is coming for a visit any minute now. My head is fighting between 'What will she be like?' and where the fibula is located. It's not a pleasant mixture.

A quiet knock on the front door sends me six inches into the air. My elbow crashes onto the table, sending a shock wave of pain up my arm.

"Ouch!" I yelp as Kate heads for the door. "I hit my ulnar nerve!" Also known as the funny bone, unless you're preparing for a science exam.

Kate stops in her tracks and looks back and forth between me and the door, unsure who to run to first. Our guest knocks again, and I nod toward the door.

"Open it. I'm okay," I say through gritted teeth, clutching my throbbing elbow. The wave of pain washes aside as Kate opens the door. I slide around in my chair so I can size up this Bailey Rand chick.

The first thing I notice is that she doesn't tap when she walks in the door; she walks like a normal person. She carries her folder against her chest, as if my records are a precious possession to protect instead of something to toss in a dark briefcase and forget about as soon as the 'Welcome to Oakville' sign fades from the rear-view mirror.

Her straight, black hair swishes around her shoulders as she bends down to take off her shoes. She sets her folder right beside her on the floor. She must be Canadian or something- why else would you take off perfectly clean shoes to walk in the house?

She looks up at me and smiles, her almond-shaped eyes open and friendly. I discreetly rub my elbow one last time and force my mouth into a returning grin.

"Hello, Taz. It's nice to meet you, I'm Bailey Rand, taking over for Moriah Cade," she says, following us over to the kitchen table.

Definitely Canadian, I decide as soon as she opens her mouth. I wonder how she ended up as a case worker in Iowa.

"So, what are your favourite and least favourite parts about Oakville?" she asks first, arranging her papers on the table in front of her.

"Uh…" That was completely unexpected. Moriah always got right down to business so she could leave as soon as possible, and she couldn't care less about my needs and wants if nobody complained.

"Well, I guess I like the school. I've made a couple friends," I finally reply, since I can't say 'the dirt bike races'.

"And what are your friends' names?" Bailey prompts.

Is this some kind of trick? I wonder. Maybe Kate told her about my little night out and is trying to figure out who could be involved. Well, too bad Kate, because I'm not admitting anything.

"Chloe and I get along," I answer with a shrug. Take that, Kate. You know Chloe would never sneak out in the middle of the night.

Bailey nods and moves the conversation along, much to my relief. "And what is something you don't like about Oakville?"

I shrug. "It's kind of small, and there are better animals than a herd of goats, but it's alright." I could add deep questions and brown-suited preachers to the list, but I keep those thoughts to myself.

"There could be worse things," Bailey says with a chuckle. "Kate is an old hand at foster care, so I know you're in good hands."

Something changes in the air, and the room falls silent. Bailey's smile fades, and she glances between me and Kate. My fingers and toes are suddenly freezing, my face is boiling, and a chill runs through my middle.

I'm not the first one. Kate has had other foster kids. That wouldn't bother me except for one thing- where did they all go? And if she didn't hold onto the others, there is no reason under the sun why she would choose to hold onto me.

This is why you never settle in somewhere, Taz. Not even a little bit.

"Uh- Kate used to do emergency foster care for- for young children," Bailey finally stammers out, looking bewildered. She knows she said something wrong, but she hasn't quite figured out what.

Kate smiles thinly. "I guess it never came up before, Taz, but yes, this isn't my first rodeo. I used to take care of small kids and babies, usually for a week or two before they got settled somewhere more permanent."

"And that's totally different from this situation," Bailey jumps in, understanding dawning in her eyes. "This is your permanent placement; not an emergency weekend getaway."

Somehow, Miss Bailey Rand has located my biggest fear and gotten straight to the heart of it. I wait for Kate to chime in in agreement, but she just nods. Her lips are pressed together in a firm line, and there's pain in her eyes. She tries to smile at me, but it comes out more like a grimace.

The feeling rises inside me, like a freight train headed down a one-way track. I *must* get out of here before the tension in the room consumes me. I shove my chair back, and it tips over with a crash as I turn and bolt from the room.

I let the back door slam behind me before running across the back lawn. I dodge the goat barn and head for the trail that winds from our property over to the Colby's place. The soft, lush grass fades into sharp gravel. The stones pierce my feet, but I welcome the pain and keep running. Tears well up my eyes, and I bite my lip hard enough to taste blood in a feeble attempt to keep them back. This is why it's best to never get attached to any place or person- sooner or later, they'll turn around and bite you. I need to stand strong, a solitary lighthouse weathering the storm that's called 'life'. Alone. The walls must stay up, whether hope can survive in the darkness or not.

I slip off the main trail onto a thin thread of dirt covered with sticks and leaves that winds off into a grove of trees. My lungs are burning for air, and there's a sharp, stabbing pain in my side, but I keep going. A few low-hanging branches slap my face, obscuring the trail ahead. Then I'm falling, knees buckling beneath me. I land on my arm on the other side of a large log blocking the trail and collapse into a sweaty, miserable heap.

I don't know how long I lie there, blocking everything out except for the sound of my harsh breathing and the mantra circling around inside my head. Don't think. Don't think. Don't think.

My head jerks up at the sound of snapping twigs nearby. I curl back into a tight ball and focus on keeping my breathing quiet. I'm not in the mood to face Kate or Bailey or anyone else for a long time.

The footsteps come closer and closer, until finally a cautious voice calls out, "Taz? Is that you?"

I groan and sit up against the fallen log. "Hi, Chase," I mumble, and silently congratulate myself for not letting any tears escape on my run through the woods. Chase doesn't need to see me dirty and crying.

He hops over the log and sits down beside me, pulling his knees up and resting his elbows on them.

"You good?" he asks, cocking his head to one side. His forehead wrinkles with concern, and I look away. I will not cry.

"Yeah, I'm good," I mutter, staring at a busy anthill on the ground nearby. Even the ants seem to know where they belong.

"Except for the fact that you were crashing through the trees like Bigfoot a minute ago," he states. He gives me a look that says he knows something is up, and he won't stop until he gets to the bottom of it.

I puff out a big breath of air and lean my head back against the top of the log. *I might as well save us both the trouble and spit it out*, I decide before answering.

"Did you know Kate used to do foster care?" I ask.

"Yeah. So?" He doesn't get it.

"So…where did all those kids go? And how soon will I join

them?" I sneak a glance over his way, and watch his expression change from confused to understanding. "Bailey- my new case worker was here, and she said…" my voice trails off.

He puts a hand on my knee and says, "Taz, that was different. She did emergency placements, for kids who needed last minute homes while things got sorted out. Then they would go live with a relative or whatever." He squeezes my knee before adding, "Don't sell yourself short. I don't think Kate's looking to dump you anytime soon. And if she does, you can come stay with my family," he adds with a wink.

I smile in spite of myself. "It doesn't work that way, Chase. You need licensing and stuff; you can't take somebody in on a dime. But thanks for trying."

He raises his chin, jaw set in determination. "Oh, yeah? Whoever made those laws hasn't tried to force them on a Colby yet." His set look dissolves into a goofy grin, and I can't help but laugh.

"Listen, it's obvious Kate cares about you," he says, his expression turning serious once again.

"Then why didn't she say so when the topic came up?" I ask, addressing the biggest worry still dancing around my brain.

Chase sighs and runs a hand through his hair. "It's a hard topic for her. She hasn't done it since her husband died, and so I'm sure it rem-"

"She was married?" I cut in. "What else do I not know about this guardian of mine?"

Chase looks at me. "She never told you?"

"No," I retort. "Do you think I would be this surprised if I'd known already?"

"Whoa, don't take it out on me," Chase says, raising his hands in surrender.

"Sorry," I mumble.

"It might have been too fresh to talk about. Charlie only died six months ago. It was a hit-and-run outside of Kalona."

As the shock of the discovery fades, my anger at Kate dissipates. Why would she tell me? As entitled as I feel right now, I guess I don't have any claim to Kate's personal past life. I just thought she would have shared such a big detail, considering that I'm supposed to be family, at least if Chase's reassurances are correct. And why are there no pictures of them together anywhere? Is there a room somewhere in that mansion that's perfectly preserved, with all his things, and even his scent lingering? Or did grief make her ship his whole life off to the Salvation Army the day after the funeral?

Okay, Taz, kill the made-up stuff. It's none of your business, I tell myself with a sigh.

"Are you okay now?" Chase asks, looking at me again with those concerned puppy dog eyes.

"Yeah. I'm good," I say, taking his hand as he helps me to my feet. The need to run has faded, but there's enough of it left to keep me on my guard.

Because what does Chase really know about Kate? A lot more than me, sure, but he can't guarantee I won't be waking up in Alcatraz tomorrow.

CHAPTER 17

I nervously tap my leg with one hand and grip the door handle with the other as Kate turns onto the road. The five-minute drive to school is now spent in awkward silence.

Kate and I have made a truce, but it's the elephant-in-the-room type. She sat me down the other night and explained her previous foster experience and the lingering sadness that makes her avoid the topic of her deceased husband. She didn't mean to hide anything from me, and she's not planning to ship me out in a few weeks. That was then, and this is now, and now is different. I'm here for keeps, and she even hinted at adoption sometime in the future, if I'm happy in Iowa.

Everything in me wants to believe her, but I'm scared. The whole episode locked down the castle of my heart once again, and all I want to do is run. If I was certain I could disappear forever into the Iowa wheat fields, I would be long gone. At least when the people taking you in hate you, you know where you belong. This up-and-down, never-knowing-how-they-really-feel stuff is exhausting.

The truck rolls to a stop in front of the red brick school, and I jump out of the vehicle. I can feel a bit of the tension draining out of me as I grab my backpack from the back seat and watch Kate drive away. The bell rings as I plant my foot on the first step, and I groan. Kate was in late this morning because one of the nannies was looking sick again, and we left the house at the time when we usually arrive at school.

Since I'm already late, I take my time wandering down to the office to sign in. Lauren is sitting in her chair, typing and writing at the same time. Her eyes dart back and forth between her computer to her notepad, while her ambidextrous fingers fly. She glances up, and a wide smile wreaths her face as her hands come to a standstill.

"Hello…Taz, is it?" She waits for my affirming nod before continuing, "Well, take a seat on that blue chair there, and tell me what's up. The principal never minds if I chat with the kids during the last week of school, and I have some extra donuts behind my desk, or caramel toffees if you'd prefer," she says, waving a dimpled hand at a ragtag collection of snacks piled on a stool nearby. "These are mostly gifts from parents or treats staff brought in to celebrate the end of the school year."

The principal shouldn't mind if she takes a few minutes off, since she's working twice as fast as anyone else, I muse as I pull a fluffy, fur-covered chair up to her desk and make myself comfortable.

"Sure, I'll take a donut," I answer, leaning my forearms on Lauren's massive desk. She rummages through the pile on the stool, sending a cascade of boxes sliding to the floor before finally coming up, out of breath. She triumphantly waves a six-pack of jelly donuts in the air before breaking the package open with a loud crackle.

"Here you go. I bought these on sale yesterday. Help yourself, although I wouldn't recommend the whole package in one sitting. I know I could do it, but my stomach is much larger than yours." She lets out a hearty cackle, the kind that makes you laugh along. I carefully pick out a donut, because it seems like the selection process is very important to Lauren. She nods in approval when I grab the largest donut, right from the middle. It's caked with powdered sugar, and jelly is bleeding out one side.

"Delicious," Lauren says seriously as I take my first bite. My mouth is full, so I just nod in agreement.

The whole situation makes me want to laugh. Here I am, supposed to be in class, but instead I'm lounging with Lauren, eating food. I love this woman.

Lauren leans back in her chair, and it emits a creaking groan. She picks up the second-largest donut and takes an enormous bite, powdered sugar floating down onto her notes. I lick the sugar off my own fingers and politely decline the blue handkerchief she offers, since the streaky cloth doesn't look like it's been washed since the start of the school year.

"That was good," Lauren sighs, swallowing her last bite. "So, are you glad that school is almost finished?"

I prop my feet up on the desk, because I somehow know she won't mind, and nod. "It'll feel good to finish." If I can get over my awkwardness around Kate.

Lauren shakes her head vigorously from side to side, making her long, dangling earrings bounce wildly. She whacks the one side of her head before looking back up at me. "Sorry, I had a bug in my ear. Now, what were we- oh, yes, school. I'll say, I'm mighty glad to be out of here. I love the kids, y'know, but summer break is just dandy."

Still reeling from the aggressive head bobs, I can only nod before she asks the next question.

"So, Taz, how are you liking Oakville? Have you been to Pop's Soda Fountain yet? They have the best root beer floats. And you must visit the grain elevator sometime. That's 'elevator' as in a building that stores grain. It has an elevator- that's 'elevator' as in a big box that's a much better alternative to stairs- that shoots you all the way up. You can see for miles from the top."

Normally, I close up when people ask how I like Oakville, because of all the inevitable questions that follow. Questions like 'Are you settling in alright?' 'We'd love to have you over sometime' and 'I have a daughter your age. I bet you could be best friends!'

But for some reason, I couldn't care less about Lauren's questions. I guess it's hard to take someone seriously when they're wearing tie-dye and bagel crumbs.

"It's alright," I respond after a moment. "I've never been to either of those places, but they sound cool."

Lauren gives another hearty nod and opens her mouth to say something, but a set of approaching footsteps causes her to sit up straight in her chair. I remove my feet from the desk and take the cue to act like a student instead of a friend.

"Um, what were you here for in the first place?" Lauren's brow wrinkles, and she squints her eyes at me.

"I need a late pass," I explain.

Lauren rummages around in one of her drawers as the footsteps get closer. I hold my breath as they stop outside the door.

"Lauren?" a deep voice asks as my math teacher sticks his head around the door frame. "Have you seen- ah. There you are, Taz. I was wondering why you hadn't showed up yet, and I didn't recall seeing a note of absence."

"I'm getting her late pass now," Lauren calls, finally coming up with a bright pink slip of paper. "Here it is, Taz. Mr. Avery, don't you have better things to do then wander the halls?"

Mr. Avery winks at me before giving Lauren a dutiful nod. "Yes, I'd better rescue the aid from my class. I expect to see you there in five minutes, Taz." With that, he strolls away.

I'm trying to figure out if it's legal for teachers to wink at students when Lauren shoves the signed slip across her desk and gives me a bright smile.

"It was fun talking with you, Taz," she says before leaning conspiratorially over her desk and whispering, "You know where I am if you're late tomorrow."

I pick up my pink slip and throw her a grin over my shoulder before trudging slowly down the hall toward math. I would love to be late tomorrow.

By the time classes let out for lunch, I'm about to explode. There's only so many 'fun' games and educational movies a kid can handle. I take the back hallway to avoid another unwanted invite from Chloe and duck into the cafeteria before the crowd gets there. The lunch lady plops a blob of mashed potatoes and a hunk of oddly coloured meatloaf on my tray before waving me on. I grab a chocolate milk from the next counter and make a beeline for one of the back tables in a quiet corner. Talia is already there, which doesn't surprise me. I could have a rocket pack on my back and still not beat her to the cafeteria at lunchtime.

She looks up from her own tray of textured mush and nods as I slide into the chair across from her.

"Got some news," she says around a mouthful of mashed potatoes.

I focus on sawing off a hunk of meatloaf and pop it in my mouth instead of answering. We play our usual game of me pretending I'm not interested and her waiting for me to ask what it's all about. I break down first this time, setting down my fork and leaning forward in my seat.

"Oh yeah?"

Two words are enough to break the ice, and she folds her arms over her chest with a small smile.

"The races are starting up again- and they'll be better this time. Frog's place has a two-acre field out back, and they've turned it into a track. And this time, the track is big enough to have a real race, not those dumb little timed things," Talia explains with a grin.

It's funny how the best small-town race is suddenly 'little' and 'dumb' once something bigger and better comes out, but I keep my thoughts to myself. The old excitement returns- that magical elixir of dangerous and daring and forbidden. I know

I'm only going to have so many lucky strikes, and one of these times I'm going to get caught for good. Kate and I have made it over so many bumps in the road, and despite how I feel about her right now, things have been going smoothly in Oakville. I can honestly say this is the best place I've ever stayed, yet the perfectness of it makes me want to gamble with my future.

At least if I ruin things, it's my fault. It hurts less to hurt yourself then to wait for other people to do it for you, I remind myself. That's been my rule of thumb through the years, and so far, it's kept me safe inside- safe from the rejection that inevitably shows up. 'We need you to pack your bags, Taz.' That's because I almost set your house on fire. I get it. At least it's not because you don't like me. That's the way I think.

Talia waves her hand in front of my face, and my eyes refocus on the school cafeteria walls.

"Calling Taz. We have a request for your brain presence here on earth," Talia teases as I push her hand away.

"Where do we meet? Here again?" I ask.

She shakes her head. "Frog's place is close to my end of town, so meeting here doesn't make sense. We can meet at my place again if you want and walk from there. There's a shortcut we can take, but its only accessible on foot," she explains, drawing an imaginary map on the table.

"Okay, cool. See you on Saturday," I say, ignoring the twinge of uneasiness in my stomach.

You'll only get so many chances, a small voice whispers inside my head.

I'll just go one more time and see what it's all about, I argue. *Talia's my best friend, and I can't let her down. This is the last one.*

Are you really going to go against Kate's wishes again, after all you've put her through? The voice is no longer small or quiet. *'Now is different. You're here for keeps.' Isn't that what she said?*

I know, but I have to go. I don't want to lose my best friend.

Besides, it would make AJ proud. He's going to think I'm becoming soft.

So, who's more important here, a classmate or the woman who feeds and clothes you and gives you a place to stay? And do you really think AJ would be proud? The old AJ, maybe, but he's changed. You can't tell me you don't see that.

I focus on a strange green morsel in my meatloaf and try to ignore the chorus of arguments circling inside my brain.

I'm going.

* * *

Which bone joins with the tibia and kneecap to form the knee joint? I scratch my head before scribbling 'femur' in the blank. Or is it the fibula? No, it's the femur.

I sigh and lay my head on top of the paper. The last exam of the year happens to be five pages long and includes a short essay, and I can't focus today. Bailey Rand is coming for try number two this afternoon, and I'm not looking forward to it. I hope she gets straight to the point this time, instead of asking unnecessary questions and pretending she cares.

I sit back up with another sigh and read the next question. What's the difference between an artery and a vein. Okay, I thought we were on bones, but we're jumping all over.

Arteries are bigger, I jot down. Good enough. Let's move on.

The exam takes an hour and a half to complete, and there are definitely a few I guess on, but I finally hand my test in a little before noon. The afternoon will be one big party, but I get the privilege of skipping it- to meet with Bailey.

Hey, I'll get to go to a real party tomorrow night, I remind myself as I grab my backpack. I wave goodbye to a few kids and head out to the parking lot. That's much better than a few cupcakes and a plastic cupful of pink lemonade.

Kate's truck is already in the parking lot, and she steps on the gas as soon as I shut the door. Her face is pinched with worry, and she keeps chewing on her lower lip.

"What's wrong?" I ask nervously. Weird vibes always make me think of all the bad things I've done lately and wonder which one she's found out about.

"I'm worried about Raven. She's not sucking well, and she's very lethargic. I tried giving her electrolytes to keep her hydrated and help her perk up, but so far there's no change."

Raven is the newest kid on the farm, an adorable black goat with a tiny white snip on his nose. After Cairo, Raven's my favourite. Kate called me out to the barn one evening last week, and I got out just in time to see Raven being born. It was kind of gross, but also cool. Poor Raven belly-flopped into this world, but Kate assured me that's normal for goats.

"I'll call the vet out tonight if he's not better by chore time," Kate mutters to herself. "He's not looking good, not good at all."

I fold my hands together and squeeze them between my knees as the vast wheat fields and big oaks flash by. Kate is supposed to be the strong, unflappable one. Seeing her worried is making me feel all topsy-turvy inside, like a brewing tornado.

At home, I slap together a few peanut butter sandwiches while Kate goes out to feed Raven more electrolytes. She comes in with slightly better news and nasty smelling clothes.

"He's definitely looking better," she says, and a few of the worry lines around her mouth smooth out. "Sorry about the smell," she adds as I automatically wrinkle my nose whenever she comes near me. "Goat diarrhea has a terrible odor."

"No kidding," I agree, pushing her plate across the counter toward her. "I'm going to go eat in the living room."

Kate smiles before gulping her sandwich down. "I'd better go shower before Bailey gets here."

I eat my own sandwich at a more reasonable pace before getting up and putting the plates in the dishwasher. Upstairs, Kate's room door slams shut, and I hear her footsteps coming down the hall above me. A gentle knock sounds on the front door.

"Come on in," Kate yells from the top of the stairs.

Bailey Rand lets herself in and pauses to unlace her shoes before greeting me with a big smile.

"How are you today, Taz?" she asks kindly.

"Good," I answer warily. This had better not be like last time. I don't need anymore family secrets uprooted or surprises coming to light.

Kate comes down the stairs and shakes Bailey's hand before leading both of us over to the living room. I sit uneasily at the edge of the love seat, the couch furthest from the easy chair Bailey situates herself in. I watch the light shimmer and dance across her shiny black hair as she opens her files and spreads them across her lap.

"How's school going?" she asks, and I groan inside. I was hoping she would cut the small talk.

"Fine," I mumble. It's going to be one-word answers, Miss Rand. Thankfully, she lets that go.

"Still having fun here?"

"Yep."

"It looks like you only have a few more hours of community service left. You're right on schedule. That's great."

"Uh-huh."

She must be a fast learner, because she moves on to the important stuff after that. I focus my gaze on her and let my brain wander elsewhere. The 'listening mask' is one I've learned to put on well. It filters out all the boring stuff, and still enters the key points into my mind's database.

Bailey spends a good chunk of time outlining all the things Moriah failed to do. I was supposed to have started some booklet thing to help me make better decisions. Bailey holds up a colourful book with a peaceful sea on it, and a bright title blazed across the top: Charting a New Course. I smile and nod and imagine chicken noises coming out of her mouth as she opens the book and shows me the different activities. They're designed to 'stimulate good behavioral choices and overall emotional well-being'. That's all I get out of her explanation; the rest sounds like squawking.

Finally, right around the point where all the feeling has evaporated from my tense legs, Bailey closes her file folder and packs up her papers.

"That's enough for today. I'll be by in about a month or so to check up on you," she says. She comes over to me, lifting my hand and wrapping it in her soft, cool grasp. "Keep your chin up, girl," she adds with a wink before allowing Kate to usher her out the door.

Okay, then. What was that supposed to mean? She couldn't *actually* care... could she?

As soon as I hear her car start, I grab the booklet and head for the stairs, intending to toss it under my bed and ignore it until someone puts me in a straitjacket and forces me to do the lessons. Kate has other ideas.

"Uh-uh," she shakes her head, holding out her hand for the book with a knowing look in her eye. "I'll take that, and we can do the lessons together sometime."

I pretend to groan loudly as I hand over the book. I know she's on to me now. Sometimes, Kate's a little too smart.

"I'm gonna go check on Raven. Do you wanna come?" she asks after shoving the book into a drawer.

I almost decline, but something makes me decide to go with her, after all. As I'm pulling on my boots, I notice what it is- the awkwardness I've felt toward Kate since the last CPS meeting is gone, out the door with Bailey Rand. Maybe social workers are good for something, after all.

CHAPTER 18

The final bell of the school year rings through the halls, echoing off the cement walls and drifting into the ears of every student. We shove back our chairs in sync, and race for the door, ignoring the last five minutes of the 'educational' film Mrs. Woodrow put on. It could have been the most action-packed cliffhanger, and we still would have raced out. No movie can compete for attention on the last day of school. This is as good as last Tuesday night, when I walked in the doors of the retirement home for the last time, until I'm at least eighty.

I tuck the little paper from Mrs. Woodrow into my pocket as I wade through the crush of students funneling through the door. She gave us each a small, personal note about what she appreciated in us. She was okay for a teacher, but I have a hard time getting sentimental about it. Shelley will frame hers on the kitchen fridge; mine will most likely disintegrate in the wash.

I reach my locker and spin the combination before opening the door. The thin piece of metal almost whacks a passing student in the head.

"Whoa there, watch where you swing that thing," he mutters.

"Sorry," I call to his receding back, but he's out of earshot.

I sigh and try to create a little bubble of space in front of me. My arms need more room to load up my backpack with the contents of my locker. Students scurry past, and more than a few elbows jab me in their haste. None of them apologize to me.

A black blur skids up beside me as Talia breaks a path through the crowd. She lifts her shoulders and widens her stance, forcing the river of kids to trickle out farther to get around us.

"Thanks," I murmur, and concentrate on stuffing papers into my backpack while Talia does traffic control. I just so get everything in, and the zipper seams stretch an unhealthy distance apart as I toss the whole thing over my shoulder.

"Let's go," I announce, following the thinning crowd of kids toward the door.

As we prepare to part ways at the front doors, Talia leans over and whispers in my ear, "Tomorrow night, my house. That'll be the real end-of-school party," she grins.

I nod. I don't feel even a twinge of sadness as I leave the red brick walls behind. It was nice knowing y'all for a couple of months, but I'm moving on now. The chances of ever stepping foot inside these halls again is slim, despite what Kate and Bailey Rand and all the rest say. Taz never stays anywhere.

As soon as I've climbed up into the truck, Kate tosses a thin book on my lap. I glance down at the title and wrinkle my nose in disgust.

"I have a hair appointment. I want to get it done before my church ladies' tea tomorrow evening. I figured you could do your first lesson while you wait for me," she states.

I sneak a glance over at her and pick the book up by the tips of my fingers. She stares at the road as if her life depends on it- which I guess it does- and pretends she isn't forcing me to dive into the worst booklet ever written- Charting a New Course.

"Or we could do it together after supper tonight," she offers with a smug smile as she turns into the parking lot for the hair salon. I could throw something at her; she knows full well I'm not doing this with her looking over my shoulder.

"You'd better finish that first section by the time I get out," she says as she opens the truck door. "I'll be checking."

I give her my best glare and mutter names at her back as she saunters into the hair salon. Then I open the dreaded book.

I turn to the first page and grimace at the title: Owning Your Mistakes. They couldn't have made it more corny if they tried.

I skim over the paragraphs about recognizing your mistakes and harmful behaviours so you can change them and read an inspiring quote about how 'my failures don't define me as a person', before scribbling in a few one-word answers. I shut the book with a satisfying smack and bury it deep in the glove box under a wad of insurance papers and tissue packets. I can always hope that Kate will forget about it, although that's not even remotely probable.

A thin black object catches my eye, and I reach over the center console to grab it. Kate's phone must have dropped out of her back pocket when she got out. I waste no time punching in the password I've memorized from covert, over-the-shoulder spy operations, and navigate through cyberspace to my email account. Two new messages pop up, one an advertisement, and one from Micah, dated from two days ago. I delete the ad and open the second email.

> to: taz4ever
> from: micdawson
> subject: re: the bro
>
> aj says he got your letter, but he might not be able to send another one out anytime soon. things are going down there, and they didn't like how much info he's putting in his letters, so his privileges are pretty scant right now. they have email in the center so you can try that route but you might want to make a new address and pretend to be his sister or something lol. he is only allowed to talk to family
> M

I erase all traces of my presence from Kate's phone before replacing it where I found it. Micah didn't give me a whole lot of information to go off, but I'm going to have to make another email address as soon as I can. He might not completely admit it, but I'm AJ's lifeline. I can't leave him alone, not after all he's done for me over the years. He's helped me out of almost two dozen 'prisons'; I can at least keep him afloat in his.

The salon door swings open, and Kate walks out a few dollars poorer and looking not that much different. I lean back in my seat and try to act bored as she climbs into the truck, pockets her phone, and starts the engine.

She turns to me and raises an eyebrow. "Get your lesson done?" she asks.

I feign surprise and answer, "Of course. Don't you trust me?"

"Would you trust you?" she asks skeptically, pulling out of the parking lot.

I stare out the window, avoiding her eyes the rest of the way home. It doesn't take much thought to figure out the answer to that question, and it bothers me.

I almost change my mind about going out tomorrow night. Haven't I double-crossed this dear woman enough?

Almost.

* * *

"Taz, have you seen my burgundy shoes? The ones with the open toe and the wooden heel?"

I brush a few crumbs off my lap and set my grilled cheese down on the table.

"Check the front closet," I suggest around a mouthful of toasted bread. Kate gets so scatterbrained when she's running late.

"Oh, here they are," she calls from the depths of the closet.

"They were sitting on the shoe rack. Thanks, Taz."

"Right where you always put them," I mutter under my breath, shaking my head.

Kate pushes back a strand of hair that has fallen out of her French knot and grabs a box of scones off the kitchen counter.

"Okay, I think that's everything," she says, spinning in a slow circle and surveying the room. She turns back to me and says, "Remember to check on Raven, Taz. He's been doing better since he's on medication, but if he looks rough, give him some more electrolytes. I have no clue when I'll be home. The deacon's wife is hosting the tea, and she loves to talk and organize little games far into the night, so don't wait up on me."

I give her a side hug and try to keep grilled cheese crumbs off her long, silk skirt before waving her out the door.

"I definitely won't be waiting up on you," I whisper to myself as the door closes behind her.

As soon as the Chevy rolls out the lane, I run upstairs and pull open my dresser drawers, spilling clothes across the floor. Since I have the opportunity, I may as well put on something decent for this race, even if Talia's the only one who will see me. I take the time to brush out my hair and lace up my favourite sneakers before rolling up a few blankets and sticking them under my bedcovers. I work the blankets into a human shape before going back downstairs to the living room. Kate will probably beat me home tonight, and it wouldn't do to have an empty bed in case she looks in on me.

It's still a good two hours until I need to leave, so I put on a show and try to keep myself from pacing. Today has been the longest day of my life, and the race can't start soon enough for me.

Finally, 9:30 rolls around. It's not quite dark, but daylight is fading and soft gray shadows hover over everything as I turn off the lights and step outside.

"This is the last one," I whisper to myself as I wheel my bike out from around the side of the house. Somewhere along the line, I've started to develop a conscience, but I won't let the guilt keep me from the 'real' end-of-the-year party.

I meant to check on Raven before I left; I really did. But somehow, it completely slipped my mind.

CHAPTER 19

"There you are!" Talia jumps up from the cracked front steps of her apartment building as I pedal up beside her.

"Sorry, I had to take a back road. There were a bunch of cars out by Lochlan's, and I didn't want them to see me," I apologize.

"It's fine. If we pedal fast, we can still be there before it starts, and if not, it's no big deal." Talia picks up the bike propped up against the steps and straddles it.

A pair of headlights moves slowly up the street behind us. A small red Mazda soon takes shape as the vehicle approaches us.

Talia presses her lips into a thin white line and puts her left foot on the pedal. "That's my mom's car. Let's get out of here."

I push off and follow her. She's pedaling furiously, and soon my legs are burning from trying to keep up. I glance over my shoulder and watch the red car pass the apartment complex before jerking to a stop and reversing at a snail's pace.

We turn into a small alley and cross over to the street that runs northwest out of town.

Off to our left, the great hulking shadow of the grain elevator rises in the distance, piercing through the dark blue sky like a sword. A coyote howls somewhere ahead of us, long and eerie, and I shiver.

A loud rumble sounds behind us, and we move over to the edge of the road as an old Black Dodge rolls past us. The driver slams on the brakes and stops in front of us. I'm ready to head for the ditch, but Talia bikes right up to the passenger window.

"What are you doing?" I hiss.

She motions me up beside her. "It's my brother," she whispers back as the window rolls down. The dark-haired driver nods at me before turning his attention to Talia.

"Going to Frog's?" he asks, leaning his elbow on the center console.

Talia nods. "I thought you working tonight," she states. "How'd you end up here?"

"My shift got switched around so some guy can have off next week, and Mom's car was in the parking lot when I got home, so I figured I'd hit up the races." An unspoken message passes between them before Talia turns to me.

"We can put our bikes in the back. You'll give us a ride, right Garrett?"

"Whatever," her brother calls with a long-suffering air.

We dump our bikes in the truck bed before climbing into the cab. I slide into the back seat while Talia snags shotgun. Garrett steps on the gas, and we roar off into the night.

"Did you talk to Mom at all?" Talia quietly asks her brother. I lean back in my seat and try to eavesdrop without looking like I'm listening.

"Yeah. Apparently she finally dumped Joe, or he dumped her, and she's back home to stay." He grunts.

"To stay." Talia snorts sarcastically. "Yeah right. She'll be gone by the end of the week."

"We can always hope," Garrett nods.

The rest of the ride is silent, except for the twang of the old 80's country playing quietly through the speakers. We crest a small hill, and a circle of bright lights glares up at us from a small property off to the right. Garrett turns in the rutted dirt lane, and stops beside an old machinery shed.

"You two better get out here. Stay out of the way, and you'll be fine. I'll meet you back here right after the last race," he instructs.

I jump out of the truck and follow Talia along the rotting wooden walls of the shed. The ground pulses beneath us from the bass as we crawl through the long, overgrown weeds to the edge of the field. Rows of trucks are lined up along one side, their tailgates down, so we slither over to the opposite side. The shark from the first race is setting up shop off to one side, and Sandy is standing like a king, overlooking the track from the back of his pickup. The new track is impressive. It's wide enough for ten bikers at a time, and criss-crosses the field in a series of berms, pits, obstacles, and treacherous corners. It's almost twice as long as the course at the brick factory, and the dirt is rolled flat and smooth.

"How is Sara Geiger going to do her thing here?" I whisper to Talia, who shrugs.

"She might be cooked," is her answer.

"She'd better not be," I mutter, curling my hands into fists. "She's the best part." She reminds me of, well, me- breaking rules, making a statement, and then running as soon as the fight hits.

Someone blinks the lights on and off to signal the riders up to the starting line. Ten of the bikers line up, while the second heat hangs back, waiting their turn on the track. I scan the surrounding area for a glimpse of black and hot pink, but the Girl with the Pink Tips is nowhere to be found.

The first race starts, and the engines whine as the bikers push their machines to the limit. Frog and Lena soon emerge in front of the pack, and race neck-and-neck over a series of jumps before sailing over a pit full of water. Frog edges ahead of Lena and claims the inside in a daring move, but the now second place rider won't give up without a fight. They scream around a corner, Lena tipping his bike down to the ground like usual, before sailing over a set of rollers like two shooting stars streaking across the night sky. Lena's bike hits the dirt a split second before Frog's, and he uses the extra millisecond of traction to zoom out in front.

Near the end of the course, another biker breaks free from the pack riding back in fifth and screams around a corner jump at breakneck speed. It's Smiley, the yellow tutu flapping in the wind around his neck. The dirt spurts up from under his tires, and a large cloud of dust envelopes him as he slides through a tunnel before squeezing in along the rail beside Frog. The burly biker has no choice but to give up his spot and move over or risk a collision. Smiley grins and gives a little wave as he roars up beside Lena and pulls a daring stunt over the last water pit before squeaking over the finish line a hair ahead of the orange-haired biker. The crowd holds its breath for a long second before erupting into a mix of cheers and boos.

"Well, that was quite the race to start us off here, folks. Coming in hot at first place is our very own Smiley!" The new racetrack has given Sandy a little more of an announcer's air, and he seems to be enjoying his role immensely.

The shark has a small smile on his face as he counts out a lot less than he took in before accepting bets for the next round.

"I want the girl! I'm putting my money on the girl!" A young college-age kid shoves his way through the crowd, holding a fistful of bills.

"Dude, she's not even here," someone sneers.

"She will be," the young guy yells back confidently as he shoves his money at the shark.

"I'll put it on her, too. Five bucks for the girl," another guy shouts, pushing toward the shark's truck.

A few others join the two at the shark's table, but most people just shake their heads and mutter insults. I cross my fingers together tightly for Sara Geiger as the second heat starts lining up.

No one notices the black shadow or the extra engine's purr amid the commotion by the track, but one moment there are eight bikers at the line, and the next moment there are nine.

Talia grabs my hand and squeezes it so hard it hurts.

"She's here!" I whisper excitedly.

Talia grins at me and shivers. Sandy waves the flag and the race starts without a fuss.

The bikers stay in a tight pack, all fighting to get ahead. The small black bike attempts to break loose, but the riders on either side press in on her, forcing her back.

"They won't let her out!" I whisper, pointing down at the track as the other bikers attempt to shuffle the Girl with the Pink Tips into the worst possible position.

The other riders are so focused on keeping the girl back that they miss a tiny breach in their defenses, and the small black dirt bike squeezes through the opening and takes lead. A larger bike gets ahead of the crowd and roars up beside her, pressing her into the inside rail. The black bike shudders on impact as the two vehicles slide together, but Sara manages to keep her bike upright and break away just in time to soar over a high jump. Her pursuer, distracted from trying to push her into the rail, doesn't hit the jump correctly and falls back into fourth place while the pink and black-haired girl soars on far ahead.

Bruno dodges in from the outside rail and passes Hotshot, a small, wrinkled woman with gray hair and unbelievable strength for her size, to take second place. He expertly grabs the inside rail on the corner jump and comes up behind Sara Geiger. The two race neck-and-neck for the finish line. I hold my breath as Sara and Bruno fight for first. Bruno edges ahead in the home stretch, and it looks like the Girl with the Pink Tips might go undefeated no longer, but she gains ground on the second last jump and manages to finish a full bike-length ahead of Bruno.

The crowd falls into a deathly silence once again, but this time it stays that way, broken only by the maniacal cheers of the few who bet on Sara Geiger. Bruno rips off his bandana and throws it to the ground, stomping it into the dust. Sara has disappeared back into the shadows where no one can touch her. Talia and I jump up and down and hug each other, not caring if we're seen by the college kids.

"She did it! She won!" I whisper before we flop back down on our stomachs.

"Well, kind of," Talia agrees as Sandy picks up the microphone again.

"The top three from each race will compete in a final heat to determine the top six racers. I think you know who you are, so line up," he yells.

The small black bike rolls up to the starting line from seemingly thin air and takes its place at the far outside. She's in the worst starting position, probably just to avoid any more fights, but I know she can do it. She must, because it would be just plain awful if Bruno or Frog walked away with the first-place cash.

"I'm putting my money on her again!" the college kid yells, pushing his way up to the shark. A few more follow him this time, but most people are either still too skeptical or too stubborn to acknowledge that Sara Geiger has talent.

Sandy waves the flag, and Sara immediately shoots out in a daring move, going for the inside rail at the first corner. She moves into second place behind Lena, who swerves in front of her right before the first jump. She moves ahead of him in a model jump over the first set of rollers while he struggles to regain his footing after a less-than-ideal corner. They race neck and neck toward the triple jump, but Lena, feeling the pressure, tries to take off too early and crashes at the top of the third jump. The other riders fly past him as he remounts his bike and makes a valiant effort to regain ground, but he stays in last place the rest of the way to the flag.

Sara manages to stay well ahead of the others for the remainder of the race, and I gasp in a lungful of much-needed air as she crosses the finish line safely. She collects her money and disappears off into the night before Lena ever makes it off the track.

"Man, I wish I could disappear like that," Talia mutters as she stares off in the direction where Sara Geiger was last seen.

"Says the girl who's managed to attend college races for years without getting caught," I tell her sarcastically, elbowing her in the ribs.

"Ow! Hey, I've never tried it with a loud hunk of machinery along. Anyway, Garrett's heading for his truck. We'd better go back to the shed."

We head back to our meeting place, not bothering to crawl this time, since everyone is too worked up about Sara Geiger to notice us. Garrett's truck is idling beside the shed when we get there, and I squish up front with Talia this time. I grab the outside of the seat so I can hop out as soon as it looks like Garrett is going to crash. He doesn't seem too drunk, but I'm not going to count my life on it.

"Did you make any money?" Talia asks her brother as we head out the lane.

"Nah, I don't really bet at these things. It's a waste," he drawls around a wad of gum. "Didn't lose any either, though."

We drive in silence for awhile, Talia and Garrett relaxed and me with one hand on the door handle and the other clenched tightly in a fist. He seems to be driving in a straight line...for now. A stop sign suddenly gleams ahead, and I gasp.

"Chill out," Talia laughs as Garrett slows to a stop and looks both ways.

"She thinks I'm drunk," Garrett says in his slow drawl. "She can't relax."

"I never said that!" I protest, edging closer to the door. The last thing I need is a fight with Talia's brother.

"You're thinking it, though," he states calmly, as if he can read my mind- which seems like a possibility.

Talia gives me a side-eyed look and says, "Don't worry, Taz. My brother's more mature than most of them. He would never put my life in danger."

Your life, maybe, but I don't think he'd care two cents about mine. At least you're along, I guess, I think, but I move my fingers off the door handle.

Talia gets Garrett to drop me off a few places down from mine. She helps me unload my bike from the back of the truck.

"Same time in two weeks?" she asks, leaning against the side of the vehicle.

I swallow hard, torn between going along with my only friend and obeying the law.

"I'll have to think about it," I finally say.

I expect Talia to say something like, "You're not a chicken, are you?" but she just nods and gives me a friendly slap on the back.

"I'll be around if you show up. Apartment 31B," she says before climbing back into the truck.

I wave at them before mounting my bike and heading down the road. A sinking feeling works its way into the pit of my stomach as I pedal in the long lane. Maybe its just the guilt again, but something doesn't feel right. The first thing I notice when I turn the corner and approach the house is the glow coming from the backyard.

The barn. Raven. I drop my bike and run around the side of the house. The porch lights are on, lighting the way out to the barn, which is mostly dark except for the left corner, where the maternity pen is.

I forgot to check her. If anything is wrong…its my fault. I swing open the door and run down the aisle, past the pens of sleepy goats to the figure bent over in the maternity pen. I don't bother with the gate; instead, I hop over the pen walls and skid to a stop in front of Kate. She looks up from Raven as I approach.

"I'm so sorry, Kate. I was going to check her, I promise. I just forgot!" I can feel tears prickling the back of my eyelids, and I furiously blink them away. "Is it really bad?" I finish in a whisper, my voice cracking.

"He's taken a turn for the worst. I'm giving him some electrolytes now, and if he's still alive by morning, there's some hope." She looks at me again, and her expression softens. "It's just a goat, Taz. Sure, it's sad if Raven dies, and we'll do everything we can for her, but it's just a goat."

"But…" My voice trails off. But it's my fault. That's the difference.

"It's not your fault, Taz," Kate says quietly, as if she can read my mind. "We all forget things."

But if it hadn't been for that stupid dirt bike race, I probably wouldn't have forgotten, I scream silently. I would have been thinking.

Kate gently pulls the nipple out of Raven's mouth and gives him a pat before she stands up. She puts an arm around my shoulder, which just makes me feel worse.

"The important part is that you're home safe. Next time you put blankets in your bed, maybe add some hair to the top. No one sleeps with their head completely under the covers," she adds. She doesn't sound mad, and I wish she would. If she was angry, at least I would know how to deal with it. You can never predict someone's next move when they act calm. It's like a lion, stealthily waiting in the shadows for the perfect chance to pounce on its prey.

I wash out the bottle while Kate puts away the medicine bottles from earlier today and turns out the lights. Then I follow her up to the house.

"Go to bed, Taz. It's after one, and Bailey Rand is coming tomorrow morning. I had to tell her. I'll only stretch the rules for you so many times."

I nod, not surprised. Kate did more than stretch the rules last time by not telling Moriah about my midnight escapade. She broke them. I slowly climb the stairs and head down the hall to my room, feeling utterly defeated.

You blew it, Taz. There's no going back now. You had another chance- and a decent one at that- and you threw it away for a couple nights of fun. You've made some stupid choices, girl, but I think this trumps them all.

I jump into bed and pull one of the rolled-up blankets over my ears, trying to block out all the noise. But its pretty hard to keep it out when most of it's internal.

At least you don't have to feel bad for AJ now, because you're headed in the same direction, I berate myself.

It's going to be a long night.

CHAPTER 20

My eyes feel gritty and swollen when I roll over in bed for what seems like the millionth time and check my alarm clock. The red numbers glare back at me: 4:22. I sigh and give up on trying to sleep. All I can think about is the helpless black goat I probably killed. I should have never started going to those races. The trouble they've brought me far outweighs the excitement.

"You know what," I grunt, swinging my legs onto the floor. "I'm gonna do it."

I grab yesterday's clothes off the floor and pull them on before tiptoeing out the door and down the hall. I sidestep the creaky floorboard right in front of Kate's room; I don't know how she'd react if she caught me sneaking around again. I'm not sure if it would matter at this point.

The house is dark and shadowy, and I run my fingers over the various pairs of rubber boots tossed across the mudroom floor before feeling the distinctive shape of my own. I hop into them and ease open the door.

The porch lights flicker on as I step outside, and I jump. I forgot the ones out back were motion sensing. The large circles of yellow illuminate the path out to the barn. I glance over my shoulder at Kate's window before heading into the barn, but the small square stays dark.

I flick on the single barn light, and a few goats lift their heads to stare at me from the murky shadows, wondering what is causing this disruption to their beauty sleep.

"Sorry, guys," I whisper, "But I don't know this barn well enough to walk through it blind."

Cairo bleats from the far pen, and I walk over and give him a little pat before heading to the maternity pen. This might be the last time I see him.

Raven hasn't moved an inch from his huddled position in the corner. From the gate, he looks as still and cold as ice. I climb in and walk over to his side.

"Please be alive, Raven, please be alive," I whisper, my heart sinking as I reach out and touch his side. It doesn't look like he's breathing, but its hard to see in the semi-darkness of the barn. He's still warm, but that doesn't mean much. I place my hand under his nose and hold my breath as a soft, warm puff hits my fingers. I bite my lip as a tear rolls down my cheek. He's alive.

Raven might be just a goat, but I still don't want him to die, especially not on my watch.

I tiptoe out of the barn and look up at Kate's room. A shadow moves, and as my eyes adjust to the darkness, I make out the shape of a face in the window. The latch whispers as she pushes it open and leans her head out.

"How is he?" she asks, her voice loud in the stillness of the night.

"Still breathing," I call back.

I can barely make out a smile on Kate's face before she answers, "He'll be fine. Go back to bed."

This time, even though it might be one of the last nights in this bed, I fall asleep almost instantly.

* * *

to: antoine_aj
from: anastasia-antoine
subject: hello

Hello my dear AJ,
This is your Aunt Anastasia, checking in on you and bringing a wave of good cheer! I hope you are doing fine, and please thank your guardians for taking such good care of you for me. I know your time in juvenile placement might feel rough but remember that it is building character for the future. Once your time is done, please come visit me, and I will buy you a cheeseburger to celebrate the man you are becoming.
Please let me know if you need anything!
Love,
Aunt Anastasia

I bite the inside of my cheek to keep my grin from splitting my face in half and hit send. Until I know how much incoming emails are screened, I'll have to play the doting aunt. AJ should enjoy reading that, and he'll figure out who it is. And honestly, if he doesn't, I should probably give up on him.

A loud knock drifts up the steps from the front door, and I quickly shut off the computer. I can't ignore the triple knots my gut is tying itself into as I take the stairs three at a time to the bottom. Bailey Rand stands at the bottom inside the door, beside a tall, imposing woman. The woman holds my fate, sealed in a brown file folder and a large black case. Neither are smiling. This can't be good.

"Have a seat at the table," Kate invites, coming over beside me and placing a hand on my back. She gives me a soft nudge, and when my feet stay planted on the floor, proceeds to propel me over to a chair across from Bailey. I want to run- no, that's not strong enough- I want to bolt, to flee, to fly. I hook my legs in the rung of the chair to keep my body still and clench my hands into tight fists on my lap.

Kate sits down at the head of the table, and Bailey sets her folder down with a soft slap. She clears her throat and folds her hands over top of the brown cardboard before fixing her dark eyes on me. The other woman just sits there, straight and tall in the wooden chair.

"So." The single word hangs in the air like a puff of smoke from a wet fire. She unfolds her hands and tents her fingers before continuing. "It has come to my attention that you broke curfew, left the premises without permission, and ultimately violated the agreement which you signed and agreed to uphold, not just once, but multiple times. How many times, we are not sure of, and I'm guessing we may never know unless you choose to enlighten us, which I don't see happening in the near future. Regardless of that number, the consequences remain the same."

She pauses again, and the silence sucks all the air out of my lungs. I imagine this is how a person might feel in the Guillotine, waiting for the blade to fall and end life as you know it.

Bailey reaches beside her chair and hefts the black case onto the table. "We have decided to stick one of these on you. And by 'we' I mean your probation officer and me. Meet Eva. She'll be the one checking your monitor from time to time."

My mouth drops open, and I snap it shut before they see. That's all? I mean, ankle monitors suck, but I thought for sure I was headed to the slammer.

Bailey must have caught my expression, though, because she smiles a little and says, "Before you get too excited, let me outline the rules of the ankle monitor. You must be in your room by ten each night, until six the next morning. You must charge the monitor at least every other day, but it's best to do it every day. It usually takes about an hour. Any abuse, vandalism, etc. to the device will result in a felony and you will be required to pay for the monitor which, I might add, costs around $600. Escape from the monitor, which is nearly impossible, will also result in a felony charge. An ankle monitor is a privilege that not everyone gets."

I don't like how she's staring in my eyes and biting off every word; it's kind of creepy. I just nod, and for once I'm being sincere. If I was a cat, I'd be on life nine by now, and I'm going to make it last as long as possible. Eva nods from her chair, her watchful eyes scanning the room.

Eva sets up the receiver and charging device before strapping the black box onto my ankle. The thin rubber strap rubs a little, and the cool black plastic feels strange and clunky when I walk, but it's not too bad. Iron bars and locked doors would be a whole lot more uncomfortable.

Before the two women leave, Bailey comes up to me and places both hands on my shoulders. She's shorter than me, so she stands on tiptoe and forces me to look at her.

"Taz, this is a privilege. Someone is out there pulling a lot of strings for you. Don't mess this up."

I swallow hard and give her a quick nod. I know I'm lucky.

I know what I should do. I should confess it all- the hidden emails and midnight escapades and deep questions and confusing situations. The biggest worry circling my brain right now is how I'm going to let Talia know that I'm not snubbing her; I can't come. Kate might not have all the answers, but she seems to have more than I do.

Instead, I sit down on the couch and open Charting a New Course to lesson three. Maybe it's stupid, but if there are a few shadows left, Taz will hide in them and fend for herself.

CHAPTER 21

"Taz! Taz! Can you come get this goat?"

I use my elbow to push my hair off my forehead and sit up. My hands are grimy from pulling weeds, and my back aches. Flowerbeds are the most ridiculous thing ever- all they do is sit there and grow more weeds than flowers. A nice pile of rocks thick enough to smother any living thing would look so much nicer. I stand to my feet and head around the corner, where Kate is waving her straw hat at a tiny black creature. It's Raven, who was recently moved to a new pen, and has been climbing up under the head rail and slipping out. He hops sideways and dances out of reach before leaping back in and snatching a nibble from a bright pink flower.

"Look at him," I laugh as he dodges Kate's hat and looks at me. He's grinning. "He's so cute!"

"He's eating my flowers," Kate scowls. "The sneaky little critter is going to decimate my plants."

"Maybe he'll eat all the weeds for us," I counter. "See, he's chomping on that ugly reddish leafy thing."

"That's not a weed, those are my coral bells!" Kate cries, leaping to her feet and chasing Raven off with a garden spade.

"Don' t hurt my goat!" I yell after her.

"Your goat?" she calls back. "When did he become your goat? I thought you despise the beasts." She comes back and plants her hands on her hips, panting. "Well, why don't you put your goat back in the barn and put a leash around his neck."

"Aye, aye," I smirk, saluting her and gratefully running off after the little rascal.

I feel like a child, scampering through the grass after a goat, of all things, and I'm hit by an insane urge to spin in circles with my hands up in the air. I dive for Raven and miss, skidding across the turf on my elbows. I get up and make another charge for the wily goat. He slows down and lets me get close before crab hopping away. At this point, he's just playing games with me. I make one last lunge for him and get my hands around his skinny middle.

"I go-" That's all I get out before Raven slips out of my arms and takes off again. I sigh and roll to my feet. I look up to see Chase make an expert grab at the goat and secure him midair, wrapping his arms around Raven's middle.

"Where did you come from?" I ask, brushing my jeans off. His eyes glance off my ankle, and I use my other foot to brush my pant leg down over the incriminating black box.

He grins. "I was coming over to return something," he says over the disgruntled squeals from Raven.

We head into the barn, and Chase deposits Raven back into her pen. I fish through a bin of odds and ends for some rope and am about to leash Raven up when Chase motions for me to throw it to him.

"Here. Instead of tying him up, let's try putting this rope under the head rail. Hopefully it will deter him, and they can still reach over it to eat hay," he says. He ties a quick knot and strings the cord down the length of the round metal head rail. Raven stands in the corner beside Cairo, flicking his tail and watching us with his intelligent chocolate eyes.

"I doubt that'll work, but it's worth a try," I say, surveying the results skeptically.

I follow Chase out of the barn, and he picks up a pair of bright red hedge clippers from the grass where he dropped them.

Kate sits up from her bent over position in the flowerbed and calls, "I was wondering where those had gotten to."

"I just borrowed them," Chase yells back.

"Yeah, like six months ago," Kate retorts. "How about you go hang them in the garden shed before they get 'borrowed' again."

I go back to the flowerbed and bend down in the dirt again. To my surprise, Chase comes over after putting the clippers away and starts pulling weeds beside me.

"Don't tell me you enjoy pulling weeds like you enjoy mucking out goat pens," I say, giving him a sideways glance.

His ears turn red, and he focuses on prying a dandelion free from the earth. "I don't really like it. But it'll go faster with two of us."

Well, I won't complain. And he's right. Before long, we finish the side flowerbed, and Kate agrees to finish the front one by herself if we go make some lemonade.

I find a few fresh lemons in a drawer near the bottom of the fridge, and Chase gets to work slicing them up. I have no idea how to make lemonade from scratch, but he seems to have the recipe memorized.

"Fill that pitcher almost to the top with water. Add a cup of sugar. Here, throw these in and add a splash of lemon juice while you're at it," he instructs. His knife is a blur as he chops lemons at warp speed before dumping a handful of slices into the pitcher. He glances at the time as he gives it a quick stir and grins.

"Three minutes and twenty-two seconds. That's a personal best! Usually when I make lemonade, Rainey slows me down by trying to steal lemon slices. She likes to eat them, rind and all."

"What is this, a race or something?" I ask, my forehead wrinkling in confusion.

His grin faded. "Me and, uh, my older sister used to race to see who could make the best lemonade in the least amount of time. It started one day when we had to make, like, ten batches for a bunch of people that were visiting. It's something I still do, even if she's not here," he explains with a shrug. He tries to act casual, but I can tell that the memories of his sister are painful wounds that haven't quite healed. I don't know what to say, so I say nothing, and just pull a few glasses out of the cupboard.

Kate comes in then, hot, sweaty, and dirty. I let her and Chase keep the conversation going as we sit around the kitchen table with ice cold glasses of lemonade.

I wish I knew what to say.

CHAPTER 22

to: anastasia-antoine
from: antoine_aj
subject: re: hello

I'm writing this fast during free time. The comms monitor is busy with another guy right now so I have a few minutes.
Taz, I got word from my brother. Things aren't too good at my aunt's. She's in up to her eyebrows in drugs and stuff, and most nights he's too scared to sleep at her place because of the fights that every party ends in.
Is there any way you can get him out, Taz? Please? I wouldn't ask unless I was desperate-you know that, right? I don't want to make this your problem, but I can't have my little brother sleeping alone on the streets, or living in that house.
The guard is coming my way, so I have to go now. I have more to tell you so hang tight for now. And keep up the aunt stuff.
AJ

The air in the room turns to lead, pressing down on my chest in a crushing heaviness. AJ's counting on me; I'm his last resort.

There are only a few people in this world that AJ would die for, and his little brother is one of them. I know this guy, and he doesn't get worried or worked up easily. And where am I when he needs me, like really needs me? Locked up by a GPS sensor in some hick town in the middle of Iowa. If only I had left those stupid races alone, I wouldn't be in this situation. If I hadn't been 'tough, no-rules Taz', there would be nothing between me and the door, and beyond that, Ottumwa. But I had to cross every line, jump every fence, and burn every bridge.

The mudroom door slams downstairs, and I exit my email account. I rub my eyes and try to look like I just got out of bed as I trudge down the stairs. It isn't that hard, considering the feelings bubbling around inside of me. Of all the useless, selfish, stupidest things…

"Oh hey. I didn't expect you to be up yet," Kate says, standing in front of me with her hands on her hips. And of course, she looks all happy and sunshiny today. "Well, I'll put some bacon on, and breakfast will be ready in half an hour. You look like you either need a splash of cold water or more sleep," she teases.

I nod numbly and go curl up on the couch. The usual noises of pans banging and utensils clattering seems extra loud this morning. Kate starts humming a cheerful song, and I grab a blanket off the end of the couch and pull it over my ears. I need to think.

Somehow, I need to get Jack away from his aunt's house without every cop in the neighbourhood coming after me. I'm already guessing Micah is a no-go, or AJ would have gone with him over me, so there won't be much help there. The other option would be to cut off my monitor, which would set off alarms and add a felony to my record. Not to mention the $600 fee, which would take me years to pay off, especially if my only source of income is sewing pajama pants in prison for a nickel apiece. I pull my knees up to my chest and slide a finger between my skin and the ankle monitor. There's a bit of room, but not enough to pull it off, which is the whole point, I guess. I sigh and close my eyes.

There is one last resort- the email address that I'm only to contact in case of extreme emergency. But AJ has that address, too, and if he hasn't pulled the plug, neither will I. For all I know that address is connected to the Italian Mafia, or worse, the police.

"Taz!" Kate yells loud enough that the sound filters through the blankets over my ears. I shrug the fleece off and roll to my feet, wishing this whole situation could be displaced so easily.

Kate says a short prayer, and I've just put the first bite in my mouth when the landline phone rings.

"I'll get it," she says pushing back her chair.

I eavesdrop on her side of the conversation, and my heart sinks as she says, "That sounds like so much fun, Chloe! Why don't you come over a little early and have supper with us, too?"

As soon as Kate hangs up the phone, I pounce on her.

"What does Chloe want?" I ask. I'm in no mood to entertain anybody.

"There's supposed to be a meteor shower tonight, and Chloe was wondering if she could come over and watch it with you from the top balcony. Her place has too many automatic yard lights and stuff around, and there isn't a nice clear spot there to watch the sky. She's coming for supper, too."

I paste a smile on my face and try to look happy. "That sounds like fun," I squeak out.

Kate raises an eyebrow at me as she slides into her chair. "You don't sound too thrilled. Why not?"

"It's fine. I'm just tired, I guess. Maybe after I wake up a little more, I'll feel like hanging out."

"Well, you've got all day to chase away the sleepiness," Kate cheerfully retorts, taking a sip of her coffee. "You can come shopping with me if you want and pick out a few snacks for your meteor party."

I almost agree to go, but a sudden idea strikes my brain. This couldn't be more perfect- a few hours to talk to AJ and think, uninterrupted.

"I'll stay here. I trust you to pick good snacks for us," I decide.

"Well, if you're going to sit here all morning, you might as well do something useful, like wash up that stack of pans from yesterday. They're too big to fit in the dishwasher; besides, it wouldn't get the crust off them well enough anyway. Oh, and…" Her eyes twinkle at me.

"I'll find stuff to do," I interrupt as I push back my chair and take my plate to the sink. There are only three pans needing to be washed, and I breath a sigh of relief. I'm not spending all morning scrubbing dishes when I should be brainstorming for AJ.

Kate takes her merry old time getting ready, but finally she disappears out the door. The minute the Chevy disappears out the driveway, I dart upstairs to the office and log back into my new email account. There's another message from AJ.

> to: anastasia-antoine
> from: antoine_aj
> subject: jack
>
> Okay, I'm back. So yeah, like I said, things aren't very good for Jack. Whatever you do, just don't go to the police. They'll ship him off to some foster family, and I'll never see him again. He can't hear, so I'm worried about what they'll do to him in state care. He can read lips and stuff, but people talk so fast these days, and he has a hard time communicating. I don't want him holed up in

some orphanage because nobody wants to trouble themselves with a deaf kid.

Before she died, my grandma told me about some friend of hers who lives west of Burlington, just across the state line in Illinois. She owns a camp for troubled families and kids to stay at. He knows the address. I need you to take him there. He can't read very well, so he'll get lost trying to take himself there even if you put him on the right bus. If the camp lady doesn't take him, or tries to turn him in, then disappear into city somewhere and we'll figure it out then.

Please tell me you can do this, Taz. Micah says he can't do it because he's tied up, and besides, he wouldn't have the patience for Jack.

Oh, and my aunt's address is 101 Smart Street.

Please.

AJ

I log out of my email account again and put my head in my hands. When did life become such a tangled mess? I was starting to get used to this place, to living instead of merely surviving. I was so close to letting down the walls a few times, but now I'm glad I didn't. I like Kate- most of the time at least, and she wouldn't be a parent if I liked her all of the time.

And now I must leave. I can't ignore one of my own kind, stuck in danger. I always had AJ; now it's my turn to be that person for Jack.

I was never as independent as I thought. Everybody needs someone when the things fly out of control. But what if that 'someone' isn't strong enough? What if I can't do it for Jack?

There are so many obstacles in the way, so many people who could get hurt no matter my decision. Jack or Kate? AJ or Chase?

Talia or Chloe? Why does everything have to involve two sides? And yet there's no one trustworthy enough to go to. Kate, or Chase, or the pastor, or the police… they'll all stick Jack on a path into state care, well-meaning or not. I have to figure this out on my own.

It feels like I'm behind the wheel, driving too fast around a curve in the road, aiming for the turnoff onto Dubuque Street. The car is spinning out of control.

I'm going to hit a tree.

Quiet footsteps patter down the hall, and I jump.

There's no way Kate is back already, I tell myself as I leap out of the chair and slide in behind the open door. Through the crack between the frame and the door, I watch a bright red beret go by, followed by a head of dark hair. I hold my breathe and hope they can't hear my pounding heart as they walk by the office, but they keep on down the hall toward the attic steps. I let out a whoosh of spent air as their footsteps creak on the wood somewhere off to my left.

How did they sneak in so quietly? I ask myself. I didn't hear a car or a door opening or anything. You're losing your street senses, Taz.

I pad back to the chair and log back into my email. I straighten my back and send a quick message before I chicken out. It's not a matter of following rules anymore; I'm going to break so many of them, including putting a felony on my rap sheet. But it's something I must do. I have to be there for the person who was there for me.

> to: antoine_aj
> from: anastasia-antoine
> subject: re: jack
>
> I got your back, my dearest nephew. Of course

I'll tell your friend Happy birthday for you! I probably won't see him until Sunday, but when I do, I'll even give him a birthday gift for you. Do you think he would enjoy bus tickets to his favourite park?
Love you always,
Your Aunt Anastasia

I send one more email off to Micah before heading downstairs and unleashing my worry on a couple crusty pans.

to: micdawson
from: taz4ever
subject: yo
What's the best way to remove an ankle monitor without detection?

* * *

"Taz, look what I found for you." Kate grins, waving a white shopping bag in front of me. I paste on a smile and shove Charting a New Course off to the side. (Can you tell I'm trying to be good?)

She pulls out a steel blue jumpsuit with a white shirt underneath and hands it to me with a flourish.

"What do you think?" she asks eagerly. "When I saw it, I thought it would be the perfect summer outfit for you.

"It's nice," I say, and not just to make her feel good. I do like it, although I have no idea where I'll wear it. I'm not planning to go anywhere this summer, except maybe Ottumwa.

Kate beams like a cat with a bowl of cream and hangs it up on a cupboard doorknob before glancing at the clock. "I'd better run out to the barn and do the chores. We'll have an early supper tonight, so you have time to get ready…oh, did you find something for lunch? I didn't expect to be gone so long."

"Madame and Parker are here painting. She came down and made us all peanut butter and jelly sandwiches," I answer, shoving my booklet back in a drawer.

"Okay, great," Kate says, whirling away to get ready for the barn.

Once she heads outside, I go back up to the office and check both of my email accounts. There's nothing new from AJ, but there's a reply from Micah, sent six minutes ago.

to: taz4ever
from: micdawson
subject: re: yo

Well, there are a few ways, none of them fool-proof (don't ask me how i know lol) you can cut the strap if its a rubber one pretty easily but that'll have the cops on your back in two seconds. you can also try and jam the gps signal with aluminum foil by wrapping the stuff around the monitor but be careful not to trip any sensors cause the more high tech ones send off alarms when theyre not touching skin for a long time. If you can manage to slip it off thats your best bet especially if its a little loose already. put a plastic bag under the monitor and over your foot then use oil or mayo or something to help slip it off your ankle. the bag will be slippery so it will work better then slipping it off skin. again, if its high tech it might trigger after a bit that its not touching skin but hopefully by then you'll be long gone.
whaddya need this for anyway? you do know its a felony to remove these things right? don't do it

unless you absolutely have to.
M

I wiggle my foot and examine the monitor. It doesn't look too high-tech to me. I grin to myself and type out a quick message to Micah.

to: micdawson
from: taz4ever
re: yo
thanks :)

As I hit send, the sound of pattering feet reaches my ears from the attic steps. I quickly log out of the computer and dive down the hall to my room. I climb onto my bed and lie down before picking up a random book lying on my nightstand and holding it up in front of my face. The footsteps come closer as I pretend to read page 44: 'So glad to hear you guys have signed up for the amazing experience of diving with sea creatures amidst the Great Maya Reef!' What *is* this book?

The footsteps stop in front of my door, and Parker peeks his head around the door.

"Hi, Taz. Do you want to see what I painted today?" he asks in his quiet voice.

I toss the book aside and jump off my bed. "Of course!" I grin.

Madame Lemair smiles at me as Parker slips his hand into mine and leads me up the creaky old steps to the attic studio. The first thing I see when I enter the room is Parker's canvas drying on the easel.

A dark cloud fills the horizon, twisting down into a long, menacing finger. The funnel dances ominously down the center of the page, heading straight for a neat little cottage tucked away on a small plot of land. A few horses pace the fence behind the house, and a dozen shingles are already flying loose from the roof. A pair of overalls spins in the air, sucked toward the rotating cloud. No one is in sight, but a soft yellow light shines from a small window in the stone foundation of the cottage. After looking closer, I can make out the shadow of three people huddled together down in the basement, waiting.

"I call this one 'Situations'," Parker says. He's still holding my hand, and my palm suddenly feels hot and sweaty in his. How does this guy get it so right every time? Does he have some inside look on my life?

"Are-aren't you s-supposed-d to t-turn the lights-s off in a t-tornad-do?" I stammer. Goodness, I can barely even talk right now.

Parker squeezes my hand. "Anything electric or with an open flame is supposed to be turned off, yes. But they have a flashlight. Everyone has tough situations. The difference is that some people have a flashlight, and others don't." He points his finger to another part of the painting, an obscure shadow. It's another cottage, also in the potential path of the twister. But this one is dark and cold.

"You don't need to see what's going on around you, but it is helpful to see what's right in front of you," Parker whispers.

I swallow hard. He's right- it would be so much easier if I could see what was in front of me. But all I can see are the dark clouds rolling in on every side, twisting around me with a dull roar.

I haven't prayed in years, but I do now. I don't know if God listens to runaway homeless orphans, or if He's forgotten about us like the rest of the world, but I give it a try.

"God, if You're listening, I could use a little light right now," I whisper as I patter slowly back down the stairs.

CHAPTER 23

I know what I must do. And I come to terms with it as I lead the way upstairs, arms laden with quilts and bags of chips. Chloe follows, chattering about the massive shooting star she saw last summer from this very same balcony with Kate. I nod and pretend to listen as we pass by the family portrait in the hallway. I wonder if Mr. Brighton ever faced a situation like the one I'm in right now.

The old wooden door at the end of the hallway creaks in protest as I shove it open. A wave of cool night air washes over us as we tumble out onto the balcony. I shiver as my bare feet hit the cold, hard wood of the high porch. The sun is setting, and the warmth of a beautiful summer day is fading faster than the light. A tower of dark clouds is gathering on the horizon, but the sky above us is crystal clear.

Kate called my probation officer yesterday and managed to extend my curfew by half an hour, but that won't mean much tonight. Even an ankle monitor can't keep me from rescuing Jack.

We spread a quilt down on the floor of the balcony and curl up in blankets. Chloe rips open a bag of chips and laughs as half of the contents scatter across our laps. I try to giggle with her, but it sounds strained, even to my ears.

I need to snap out of it. I might never see Chloe again, and I could at least thank her for her friendship attempts by zoning in for a few hours.

The pinks and purples and oranges of the sunset fade into a dark indigo, and little pinpricks of light start appearing across the sky. We lie down on our backs, and Chloe helps me find the Big Dipper, and Orion, and the North Star. A shooting star streaks across the sky, putting on a brief show of dazzling sparkles. I stare up at it and make a wish.

The wind picks up, and I huddle deeper into my blanket. A few small clouds skid across the stars above us, and the tower to the west moves closer.

Chloe seems oblivious to the coming storm.

"So, what do you think of Oakville by now?" she asks, grabbing another handful of chips.

I shrug and give some generic answer. I can't do deep conversation right now, but I appreciate her caring.

A few large raindrops splatter on top of us, and Chloe finally takes note of the weather. We can't see the stars anymore, anyway, so we pick up the blankets and rush inside as the rain increases to a steady drizzle. I glance at the time at we drag everything down to the kitchen. So much for extending curfew.

Kate mixes up some hot chocolate for us, but all I can think about is the leaving. Chloe needs to leave, so I can leave. The plan must go forward tonight, rain or shine.

Kate and Chloe try to draw me into easy conversation, and I play all the parts and say the right lines, but it's all an act. Finally, fifteen minutes before ten, a black Dodge truck pulls into the driveway.

"Chad Dad is here. I'd better go," Chloe says, rinsing her mug out and placing it beside the sink. "Thanks for having me over, Taz."

She gives me a hug, and I hug her back for dear life. This might be the last time, and despite all the times I pushed her away, she did try to be a good friend.

"Bye, Taz," she calls over her shoulder as she heads for the door.

"Bye, Chloe." *I wish I could tell you this is the last goodbye*, I add silently as she disappears into the rain.

Kate rinses her own cup out and stretches.

"Well, this old lady might head to bed," she says with a yawn. "You might as well take advantage of your extra half hour. Make sure you're in bed by ten-thirty."

I nod and take another sip of my lukewarm chocolate. I let her hug me goodnight and tell her I'll take care of the blankets before she disappears up the stairs.

Finally, I'm alone.

I wait until I hear the shower running before dumping the rest of my hot chocolate down the drain and gathering the pile of blankets in my arms. I stop by the fridge and grab a jar of mayonnaise, hiding it in the folds of the quilt, and a disposable shopping bag from Kate's collection before tiptoeing up the steps. I neatly fold the blankets and stash them in the hall closet, before going to my room and shoving the other items under my bed. The water is still running in Kate's bathroom, so I take a chance and tiptoe to the office. The chair squeaks as I sit down, and my heart leaps to my throat, but the rushing water keeps going, hiding the sound.

I quickly log into my email and check for any new messages. There's nothing.

I type a single word out in a message to AJ, regardless of the consequences. He needs to know.

Tonight.

I hit send.

The water has turned off in the shower, and I turn off the computer as footsteps head for her room door. I jump up and walk over to the small bookshelf along one wall. I hear Kate move past the doorway and down the stairs, and I edge out of the office and down the hall to my own bedroom. I shut the door and slip into a pair of track pants and a dark T-shirt before crawling under the covers.

Kate comes back up the stairs and knocks on my room door.

"In bed already, Taz?" she asks, sounding surprised that I'm not taking advantage of my extra half hour of freedom.

"Yeah, I'm pretty tired," I call back, and she moves on to her room.

I sit up in bed and grab the sage green blanket from across the end of it. I can't lie still with the amount of adrenaline coursing through me right now. I amuse myself by counting the tassels on the blanket and make it to two hundred and fifty-four before a light snoring noise drifts from the room next door. I throw back the covers and slide out of bed. A thin sliver of moon shines a feeble light across the room as I grab the jar from under my bed.

I almost laugh at the ridiculousness of it all. I'm counting on a jar of Hellman's to get me out of a highly specialized piece of technology that's designed to keep me in it. For all I know, Micah's lying, or has no idea what he's talking about, and I'll be found sitting on my bedroom floor with a mayo-smeared ankle and a red face. But I'll take that risk, because it's the best way.

I crack open the blue lid and wrinkle my nose at the smell. I like mayo, but not in the middle of the night when my nerves are sizzling and I'm about to commit a felony. I dip the tip of my index finger into the cold, white substance and shiver. From now on, I know I will always associate the smell of mayo with this night.

I slide my finger under the rubber strap and stretch it out a few times before pulling the plastic bag over my foot and working it under the ankle monitor. It rustles loudly in the stillness, and I hold my breath. I will not be busted by the noise of a shopping bag.

Next, I rub some of the white goo under the rubber strap and on the lower part of the bag. The stench of mayo fills the room and overpowers everything else. I slide the bag back and forth and use my other foot to push the monitor down. The hard plastic bites into my skin as I work it over my heel, and I clench my teeth against the pain. Then, with a soft pop, its off.

I'm so happy I could cry as I pull the bag off my foot and turn it inside out. I toss the monitor inside and throw the whole thing back under my bed. The whole room still reeks of mayo, but I don't notice it anymore. I pull on a black hoodie and take one last look at myself in the mirror, almost surprised that I still look the same. Same slightly wavy brown hair and defiant dark eyes, though the fire has faded from them. I take a breath and let it out slowly, flexing my fingers to calm my nerves. The minute I step out of this room, it's over. I can't come back. I'll never see Kate, or Chase, or Talia again. I might even miss the goats. It's the finality of it all that makes me pause, but only for a little. Because my people need me.

I open the door and sneak down the stairs, out the side door, and onto the driveway. A torrent of rain pelts my face, soaking me to the skin. At least the storm will decrease visibility, a plus for me. Right now, I need to focus on getting to a bus stop. The ones in Oakville will be too risky, but there's a dumpy old shack of a stop, halfway between Oakville and Staten, run by an ancient blind man. I remember passing it on a random shopping trip with Kate. If that one's closed, I can head to the one outside of Oakville on the main drag.

I leave the old blue bike behind. It would be faster, but after everything else I've done to Kate, I don't need to add theft to my list, even if the item is twenty years old.

The gravel crunches underfoot as I walk out the long lane and onto the road. I keep my eyes and ears open for headlights and engine noises, and try not to think about, well, anything.

It'll take a miracle to pull this off. The realization hits me like a brick, smacking me square in the face before dropping down and settling in my stomach. Fourteen-year-old girls don't escape from GPS monitors and roam the countryside and travel eighty miles without getting caught. It doesn't happen.

When you're forced to stare life in the face, you realize there must be Someone bigger out there. There must be, or else there's no way you're getting out of this on the winning end. A tall pastor in a brown suit once said that, and now I know it's true. Someone is up there. And right now, I'll do whatever I can to get His attention.

"God, I tried this once already, and You didn't seem to answer, but if You really care, can You please make this work out… somehow? I don't care if I end up in jail if Jack makes it out okay," I whisper in a frantic plea.

The rain slows to a soft drizzle, and I push a strand of wet hair off my face as I continue trudging down the soft shoulder.

The whine of an engine cuts through the night, and I dive into the wheat field on my right as a small motorcycle crests the hill in front of me. The bike slows to a stop up on the road, and I realize too late that my shoe is still sticking out of the field. I pull my knees up to my chest and curl into a ball. I hold my breath as the bike shuts off.

"Hey, do you need help?" It's a strong, steady, female voice, and somehow, I know who it is. I crawl back out of the muddy field and walk towards the black and pink figure standing on the road. She takes her helmet off, and her dark hair falls around her shoulders. I can see the hot pink tips in the glow of her headlight. Her coat is slick with water, but it must be waterproof, because she looks warm and cozy, unlike me. I'm covered in mud and shaking like a leaf.

"I guess I could use a little help," I say, relief washing over me. I look up into a pair of light gray eyes, which look familiar for some reason. But I guess after you spend months trying to discover the identity of someone, anything about her might seem familiar.

"I'm Sam," she says, tucking her helmet under one arm and shaking my hand with the other. The top of her head is still dry, and the now occasional rain drops roll right off it.

I tilt my head to one side and give her a look. "Is that your real name? Cause mine is Taz, or Anastasia if you want to be my enemy."

She tilts her own head to the side and gives me a small smile. "Yep. Or, if you don't want help, you could call me Samantha. According to my license, I'm Sara, so I guess you could call me that, too."

"Could you give me a ride to the bus station between here and Staten? Or, better yet, Ottumwa?" I ask, not really expecting her to jump on the last part of my request. I don't bother asking her why she's biking around at almost midnight. Sam makes her own rules.

She shifts her weight onto one leg and nods. "I could probably swing by Ottumwa. It'll be a little tight on this one here," she adds, giving the seat a slap, "but it's better than my dirt bike."

I swallow an unexpected swell of emotion and nod. "Thanks… Sam," I say. It feels weird to finally know the real name of the elusive biker.

Sam gives me her helmet, and I slide on behind her. The seat is wet, but so am I, so I don't mind. Her place is only a few minutes away, so we take a detour and stop in for another helmet.

"If you want, you can come inside and change," she offers as we roll to a stop in front of the old blue trailer.

I nod my thanks and follow her up the sagging wooden porch and into the house.

The inside looks surprisingly modern, with dark walnut cupboards and white walls. She leads me to her bedroom and pulls out a pair of tech pants and some sort of fancy hiking shirt for me. The tag on it says 'moisture-wicking, waterproof, wind breaker T-shirt', and I wonder how much it cost as the cool fabric settles over me.

I find her in the kitchen, mixing up a protein shake in a water bottle. She nods toward a blue and black motorcycle jacket draped over the back of a chair, and I try it on. It fits perfectly, like the rest of her clothes.

She snaps a lid on the bottle and tucks it under her arm before leading the way to the door. I'm learning that Sam is a woman of few words.

"Hey, would you do me another favour?" I ask hesitantly as we approach the bike. The rain has stopped completely, and I use the sleeve of my jacket to wipe the seat down before climbing on.

She nods wordlessly.

"Can we stop by an apartment on Smith Street? I know its on the opposite side of town, but…"

"It's no trouble," Sam calls over her shoulder as she accelerates out her driveway.

I huddle behind her as we head back into the night. Sam knows every back road and cow path in the country, and she makes good time getting back to Oakville. We come in the back way, and Sam parks in the alley beside the old, desolate apartment building where Talia lives. I think the only true friend I've had here deserves a goodbye.

The front door is unlocked, and the clerk's desk is empty this time of night. I walk down a short hallway to the mailboxes and study the rows, searching for the H's. Hallen, Harper, Harrison… there it is. There are three Hayes families living in the building, but unless the apartment is under Talia's mom, my best bet is Apartment 315B- G. Hayes.

I follow the signs to the elevator, which happens to be down a long hallway beside a cavernous pool room. Through the cracked windows surrounding the pool, I can make out an inch of sludge in the bottom of the concrete-lined hole. No one has swum in that thing in a long time.

I press the second floor and eye the camera blinking in the corner. Hopefully, this place isn't manned all the time. Actually, I know it isn't, or I wouldn't have been able to walk in. My guess is the landlord lives in a Manhattan penthouse and rolls in as much dough as possible at the cost of the less fortunate. Security isn't a necessary expense, right?

The elevator stops at the second floor, and I hop out. Rows of dull brass plates mark the doors, and I follow the numbers down the hall to 315B. I hold my fist over the door and wonder what I'll say if Garrett opens it, but I knock anyway.

Only silence answers me, so I knock again, louder this time. A yell sounds from the apartment next door before I finally hear footsteps stumbling toward me from inside 315B. A sleepy Talia opens it, and peers out at me from beneath a curtain of disheveled hair. She's barefoot, in a pair of frayed cotton shorts and an over-sized T-shirt, and her eyes blink slowly as she takes it all in.

"Taz? Is that you?" she asks finally as her eyes and brain finally connect.

I stick my hands in the pocket of my hoodie and shuffle my feet. "I came to say goodbye. I'm leaving," I say.

"Wh-why? When? How?" The questions tumble out of her all at once.

"I can't explain everything, but I have to go. To Ottumwa. Someone needs help," I explain earnestly. I would tell her everything, but the clock is ticking. It's not a trust issue, it's a time issue.

"B-b-but I thought you were on house arrest," she sputters, eyeing my ankle with the blank stare of someone who's still half asleep.

"How'd you know that?" I ask. I haven't talked to her since that fateful night.

"I heard," she shrugs.

"Well, I got out."

"That's a felony, Taz!" she whispers fiercely, grabbing my arm.

"I know. I know. But I had to. I need to go help someone. I have to leave, Talia. I came to tell you goodbye," I answer urgently.

She grabs me in a crushing hug, and we stand there for a bit, in the middle of the threadbare carpet. Playing the game of 'don't let them see your weaknesses' doesn't seem important right now as I feel Talia's tears drip down onto my neck. I pull away first, and she steps back, angrily swiping at her cheeks.

"You were the best friend I ever had, Talia," I say, looking into her dark eyes.

She nods and gives me another quick hug. "I'll miss you," she whispers.

I turn back and wave to her once before the elevator doors close behind me. She looks so lonely, standing there in her pajamas in the middle of the dark hallway.

I wish it wasn't this way, but I'm glad I got to say goodbye. At least the gray car is gone from the parking space in front of the building.

I climb back on the idling bike, and we disappear back into the shadows.

I watch the dark houses fly by and remember my prayer right before Sam picked me up. Maybe God does care about me. He sent me a motorcycle, right? And a chance to see my friend one last time.

An oncoming car briefly showers us with blinding light before we slip back into the shadows left behind. Soon, the outskirts of Oakville are miles behind us.

We stick to the main road, despite the heavier traffic. After the rain, all the dirt roads will be reduced to puddles of mud, and we'd both rather not be covered in filth when we drive into Ottumwa.

The neon red sign from another bus station glows in the dark, and I squint at the numbers on the huge digital clock. It's been an hour since I snuck out of the house. If it wasn't for Sam, I'd have just arrived at the dumpy shack between Staten and Oakville.

We drive by a small cow path, barely big enough for two cars to pass each other. A pair of yellow headlights stare at us like the eyes of a preying cat.

The car pulls out behind us, and a pulse of alternating red and blue washes over us. Sam swears and veers over to the side of the road. There's a sinking feeling in the pit of my stomach as the police cruiser pulls in behind us.

"How fast were you going?" I whisper to Sam as she lowers the throttle to a soft whine. This might still work if he doesn't ask too many questions.

"I wasn't speeding," she whispers back.

A tall figure walks up beside us and shines his light at us. I get a glimpse of his face, and I know it's all over, speed trap or not.

It's the cop who arrested me.

CHAPTER 24

"Get off the bike," he commands, jerking his chin at me.

I slowly pull my helmet off and extract myself from my cramped position on the seat. What is Officer Rhoydes, according to his name badge and my faint memories, doing here, over an hour from Ottumwa? Isn't this way out of his jurisdiction?

Sam slides off the motorcycle too and puts the kickstand in place before taking off her helmet. She reaches into a small box and pulls out her license. She hands it to him and asks in a calm, clear voice, "How are you doing, officer? I wasn't speeding, was I?"

She's trying to get the attention off me, and I eye the surrounding area. The field of wheat behind me might offer some cover if I duck down low enough. Probably not, though. Rhoydes seems to sense my thoughts and dashes any hope of escape by clamping a strong hand on my shoulder before forcing me to his side.

"No, your speed was within the limit. Are you aware that assisting a minor in escaping from house arrest is unlawful and could result in federal charges?" he asks, glancing at her license. His cool tone makes me want to punch him. Sam isn't the bad guy here, mister.

Sam feigns shock so accurately I almost wonder if she knows I'm a runaway. But of course, she does. No teenager heads off to Ottumwa in the dead of night for fun.

"A-a what, Officer? I'm sorry, I don't understand. This young woman was hitchhiking along the road, so I offered to give her a ride. She told me she was twenty-three," Sam stammers, eyes opened wide in innocence.

Rhoydes narrows his eyes at her, and I can tell he doesn't quite buy it, but he just nods and hands back her license. "Alright, then. Have a good night, Miss Geiger. Taz, you're coming with me."

The rock-hard grip on my shoulder tightens, and I hand my helmet to Sam. We lock eyes as she takes it from me, and silent apologies pass between us. Her gray gaze is a familiar mix of concern and something unreadable. Where have I seen it before?

But there's no time to think about it as Rhoydes turns me around and propels me toward the police car. The red and blue lights hurt my eyes, and I can feel a headache coming on as he opens the passenger door.

He sighs and spins me around before slapping a pair of handcuffs on my wrists.

"Sorry, kiddo. But I don't trust that you won't try jumping out of my car at a stoplight," he says as the cold metal bites into my skin. He leaves them on the loosest setting, but they still pinch as he pushes me down into the car. He walks around to the front of the cruiser and leans against the hood to make a phone call. I sit there, wondering why I'm in the privileged seat of a partner instead of in the back where I belong. Then again, he never actually told me I'm under arrest. This whole thing is bizarre.

I lean my head back against the seat and whisper, "I'm sorry, AJ. I failed the mission. If they let me have one phone call before they ship me off to who-knows-where, I'll call you. And if they don't…well, I'll find some way to tell you. Because you're right—Jack needs help. And I'm sorry I couldn't get to him."

The car didn't make the curve. I've hit the trees. And here's the worst feeling of all- there's no one here to save me. Everything I've built my life on, the running and independence and loneliness, is turning out to be a lie. I can't do this on my own; I'm not going to make it.

Rhoydes slides into the driver's seat and glances at me, my head against the seat and back arched around my cuffed hands.

"You know what," he says, slapping his hands against the steering wheel, "How about we do this."

He instructs me to lean forward, and I hear a soft click as the handcuffs open. He removes the cuff from my right wrist and attaches it to the seat belt.

"There. You're going to have to rip that belt out to escape, which isn't likely to happen, and I'll notice if you try taking that left cuff off."

"Thanks," I mutter, settling back into the seat. This man is like a cross between a Labrador Retriever and lion. One minute he's ready to bite my head off, and the next he's seeing to my everyday comforts.

It takes me a total of three minutes to work up the courage to ask him if I'm under arrest. I should be, but he never said so.

He gives me a look and says, "I'll answer that question when you're ready to start talking."

I clamp my mouth shut and stare straight ahead after that. I'm not ready to spill the beans to this guy.

Soon after that, we enter the quiet streets of Oakville. Everyone's in bed, like I should be, as we park in front of the small gray stone building near the edge of town that holds the local office of the Iowa State Police. The station is dark, except for a few lights on upstairs. Either someone is working super late or super early.

Rhoydes unlocks my handcuffs and lets me out of the car. He puts an arm around my shoulders, but it's not a nice gesture of comfort. He's still scared I'll run away.

But for the first time in my life, I don't even want to run

away. Running doesn't solve anything, and eventually, your problems always catch up to you. And when they do, they hit hard. Problems tend to pick up speed as they chase after you.

Rhoydes guides me up the concrete steps and into the semi-darkness of the station. A few motion-sensing lights flicker on, providing enough light to cast eerie shadows over the empty front desk. We walk back a long, dark hallway to a flight of narrow stairs, our footsteps echoing through the building. Rhoydes pushes me in front of him up the steps, which end beside a lounge. The door is shut, but a thin beam of light spills out from the crack under the door. Rhoydes leads me past it to a small office.

He shuts the door behind us and flicks on the light. I blink furiously as my eyes adjust to the sudden brightness. He motions me into a padded leather chair and takes a seat behind the dark wooden desk. I shrug out of the stiff biker's coat and sit down. This feels like some unofficial debriefing in the basement of the White House, which would be cool except I'm the one being convicted for treason. He leans back in his chair and crosses his arms over his chest, his green eyes fixed on me.

"So, we can do this a few ways. I can place you in custody for the night and we can resume in the morning, or we can start talking now," he says, staring at me intently. The hard lines on his face have softened a little and a hint of a reasonable person shine through. But you can never trust the nice cops, especially when they keep switching personalities.

"Am I under arrest?" I ask bluntly. It's a stupid question - of course I'm under arrest- but Rhoydes hasn't actually told me so. He's being confusing.

He hesitates and sits up in his chair before answering. "Kind of. The minute you get up and head for Ottumwa, I'm booking you. But if you're willing to talk it out, we can come up with a better solution."

I stare at him. A million questions are circling around in my head, but the only one that comes out is "Why?" Didn't this guy make it clear that if I ever broke the agreement I signed, he would take great pleasure in personally escorting me to a detention center?

He attempts to smile, but it's more like a wry twist of his mouth. "Because there's a reason. Your friend is in jail right now, Taz, and unless you were taking the extra long route to Casings to get him out, there had to be another reason you left.

"Juvie isn't going to help someone like you. If anything, it will make you worse. Locking a child up because they did something bad, without addressing the circumstances behind the action, does nothing to change them. And if we don't give you the tools you need to lead a better life, you'll end up back behind bars. And while there are people who genuinely want to help troubled kids, most programs are underfunded and understaffed. They don't have nearly enough room or manpower to help the overwhelming number of kids who need them. I can't help every kid, Taz, but I can help you. You can fight me until you're on a bus to Alcatraz, and I'm a stubborn guy when I want to be, or you can take this chance and make something of your life. What's it going to be?" His voice has risen with emotion, and I know this guy's the real deal. Either that, or he belongs in Hollywood.

"But why do I get this chance?" I'm struggling not to cry at the unfairness of it all. How can I live the rest of my life in a small town drinking sweet tea when Jack is alone in Ottumwa and AJ is stuck in Casings? "Why did you pick me, and not AJ as your poster child? We did the same thing!" Hot, angry tears spill over onto my cheeks, but I don't even care.

Rhoydes pushes back his chair and stands up, leaning over the desk. "Listen, I'm doing all I can to get your friend into a halfway house. There's some stuff going on at Casings, illegal stuff, and he doesn't belong there. His trial should have gone through ages ago. But I can only pull so many strings at once, and Kate needed you. Since her husband died, she's lost her vision. She used to love helping kids at risk, and that seemed to die with Charlie. She's my sister, if you haven't figured out yet; a Roydes much longer than a Brighton. When I saw you, and heard about your situation, I knew you'd be perfect for each other. And you have been. She needs you, Taz, and if you're honest with yourself, you need her too. Don't-"

A cold wave washes over me, blocking out the rest of the words.

"You don't want me. You never did." The words coming out of my mouth with a quiet, icy firmness surprise even me. Rhoydes stops mid-sentence and stands there, mouth half-open. "I'm just another tool. As long as I keep your sister out of depression, you'll fight for me," I continue. "But what happens if I settle in, and Kate takes a turn for the worst? You want to help kids? Well, here's a light bulb moment- don't use them as your sister's therapy dog."

I spin on my heel and run for the door, ignoring Rhoydes' protests in the background and, once again, the possible consequences. Everything is falling apart.

"Wait, Taz! Let me expl-"

I race around the corner and charge down the stairs. I hear a door open somewhere above me, but I ignore it and explode out the front door and into the cool shadows of a dawn beginning. Everything is still, except for the pounding of my feet on cement as I turn the corner onto the sidewalk. I don't know where I'm going or what I'll do; all I know is, I must get away from this crushing pain inside my chest. Because I really *had* begun to believe, even if it was only for a few minutes, that Kate not only loved me, but wanted me. And that kind of let down is the hardest to bear.

I feel like a candle, just starting to flicker, before a big hand came and closed over me, drowning out the light. 'It's better to have someone when the bottom drops out,' they say. I even said it. But not when those very same people are the ones pulling up the nails as the floor creaks beneath you.

Another set of pounding footsteps registers in my ears, and I push myself harder. My lungs are burning, but the pain is far better then letting Rhoydes catch up to me. I cut across the road and head into the park. My feet slide on the wet grass as a voice calls out my name.

"Taz! Wait!" It's not Rhoydes. It's Chase. Why he's out at four in the morning is beyond me, but I don't have time to figure it out before he grabs my arm. We both tumble to the ground and go rolling across the bright green carpet of the park.

I leap to my feet and turn on him, panting. "What are you doing here?" I growl, not because I'm mad at him, but because it's easier that way.

"Don't run, Taz. Please don't run," he says, holding his hand out to me like you would to a shivering puppy.

"Do you understand?" I yell back, the hot tears coursing down my cheeks again. "I'm not wanted here! I'm no more than a pawn in Rhoydes's game. They don't want me!"

"That's not true, Taz! I don't know what Trey- Rhoydes- all said to you, but Kate has been wearing holes in the floor of the conference room down at the station since she discovered you were gone. She wouldn't be doing that unless she cared." His gray eyes are dark with feeling, and a bit of the anger and hurt drains out of me.

"But Rhoydes said-"

"I don't care what Rhoydes said. He's not your parent, or your next-door neighbour, or even your friend. But Kate and I are, and we want you to stay! And even if we didn't, even if no one in this world wanted you, God still would. He says you're worth dying for."

I want to believe him, but I've been broken too many times in the last few hours.

"What do you want from me?" I ask desperately. My teeth are chattering, and I wish I would have kept my coat on.

"I don't want anything," he says. "Neither do Kate or God, except for you to come home."

"It's too late for that," I croak out, my voice breaking mid-sentence. It doesn't matter anymore. Rhoydes can be right, Chase can be right, they can all be right. But whether they love me or not, I'm headed straight for the tank. And as for God, well I hope He hangs out behind bars, too.

A marked car pulls up beside the park, and my shoulders droop. Chase puts his arm around me, and I lean on him for a second of support. I'm exhausted, empty.

Chase hangs back as I climb into a police car for the second time tonight. Rhoydes looks at me from across the center console and sighs.

"I'm sorry, Taz. That didn't come out right," he says, his hands rapidly tapping the steering wheel. "I'm not very good at this kind of stuff, but I didn't mean it like that. Yes, Kate needs you. But we need you, too. And you need us." He runs a restless hand through his light hair. "You know, I've been there. I was the 'bad kid', always trying to get attention from my older sister. She was the smartest, the nicest, the cutest, the most helpful. She was always better at everything. I was the rebellious younger brother.

"It took an encounter with the law and a few good talks with my pastor to set me straight and get me back on the right road. If it hadn't been for Pastor Chris and Officer Hamilton, I don't know where I'd be today. Both showed me more grace than I deserved, and I want to pass it on."

I lean my head back against the seat as he takes a deep breath and pulls out onto the road.

"I'll admit, this is a little bit about Kate. I did want to help my big sister. But I want to help you, too. More than you think."

I watch the buildings flash by and think about what he said. It's kind of hard not to believe a man who ran all over the country and probably risked his position to call in every favour in the book for me. If only AJ hadn't asked me to avoid the police. Would Rhoydes really put Jack in the system? Can I trust him to listen and do what's best- for everyone? Can I tell him everything?

Running is safe. Opening up is scary. But I guess I'm going to have to be brave and do the scary things to find my way home. Because I can't do it alone.

CHAPTER 25

Officer Rhoydes puts the car in park in front of the police station and unbuckles his seat belt.

"How did you find me?" I ask as his hand closes over the door handle. There are so many questions burning inside of me, and as the adrenaline dissipates, they all come crowding to the surface.

Rhoydes chuckles and puts a hand on my arm. "That's a long story. How about we head up to the lounge, and we can talk about it there. Kate's anxious to see you."

The sun is starting to peek over the edge of the horizon, and the sky is awash with shades of pink and orange. I slide out of the cruiser and follow Rhoydes through the station. The door to the lounge bursts open as I top the last step, and Kate comes rushing into the hall.

"Did you find her, Trey?" she asks breathlessly before catching sight of me. She throws her arms around me in a bone crushing hug, but I pull back as an icy wave of reality hits me.

"D-do you still want me? After everything I've done?" I ask earnestly.

She places her cool hands on either side of my face, her eyes brimming with tears.

"Taz, I'll always want you. What you do doesn't change my love for you."

She wraps her arms around me, and I lean into her embrace. I'm crying, she's crying, Rhoydes is probably crying, but no one cares.

And yet it's not enough. Everything they did to bring me home wouldn't have worked unless Someone was answering prayers and opening doors. There's a prodigal-size hole in my heart, and only God can fill it.

"I'm sorry," I whisper against Kate's shirt, but it's not to her. And suddenly, it doesn't matter if the whole world falls apart or I have to leave, because I belong, in all the most important ways.

Kate steps back and wipes the tears off her own cheeks before putting an arm around me and leading the way into the lounge. We sit side by side on the brown leather couch, my head on Kate's shoulder. Rhoydes clears his throat and pretends nothing emotional happened. He pulls a wooden chair over from the small kitchenette in one corner and flips it around before resting his arms across the back of it and giving us a lopsided smile.

"Alright, Taz, give me all your questions," he invites.

"How did you find me? Did the monitor go off? And why is Chase here?" The questions come gushing out one after the next, and Rhoydes holds his hand up with a laugh.

"One at a time, kiddo. But here's what happened: Kate woke up a little before eleven and couldn't go back to sleep, so she decided to get up and email a friend of hers who lives in Puerto Rico. When she turned on the computer, your account came up."

I gasp. "I never logged out! I heard Kate coming last night, so I shut the computer off, but I forgot to get out of my email!" Which means...I leave the thought unfinished in my head as Rhoydes goes on.

"Lucky for us," he adds, "Kate read through them all and immediately called me. I contacted the force here and headed up this way. Technically you're out of my jurisdiction, but I've been handling your case. Kate forwarded all the emails and your other account to me, which I got a buddy to unlock. So, I knew you were headed to Ottumwa. I figured you'd be too smart to take a bus out of Oakville, and my two predictions were on McGrew outside of Staten and Lansings outside of Oakville. The bus doesn't go out of McGrew until six, so I figured even if you went there, you'd eventually head to Lansings to catch a night bus. I waited for you on the side road just before the Lansings bus station. I had another officer posted by McGrew, and if you managed to slip by both of us, you'd get caught in Ottumwa. Officers are securing that property right now, and Jack is in safe custody."

A cold chill runs down my spine, followed by a sinking feeling in the pit of my stomach. I think I can trust Rhoydes, but how can I be sure? It doesn't matter anymore, though. He holds all the cards.

Rhoydes is looking at me intently, and I fell like he's trying to read my thoughts. "Jack is going to be fine, Taz. We're still working through all the details, but the hope is to get him to stay at a camp just over the state line in Illinois, west of Burlington. Sound familiar?"

I sink back into the couch cushions and haul in a deep breath. It will work out, even if it's not the way I'd planned.

"I'm also working to get AJ into a halfway house in Kalona. The details are finalized, and it should be through court by the end of next week."

"What about…" I'm almost too scared to say it, but it's the elephant in the room for me. "What about all the rules I broke? Taking my ankle monitor off and everything?"

Rhoydes sighs. "You'll have to go through court for that one, I'm afraid. But there are a lot of people willing to vouch for you. The judge will consider the circumstances, and my guess is that you'll get more community service hours." He winks and adds, "I'll have to talk to the chief here about getting you to weed the flowerbeds out front."

I give him a wobbly attempt at a smile and move on to my next question. There's no use worrying about a court date when I can't do anything to change the outcome except follow the rules.

"Did you get Moriah moved to a new spot?" I ask, giving him a suspicious look.

He laughs, cheeks turning pink. "I may have had a hand in that, indirectly, of course." He winks at me. "She wasn't a great it for you." He pauses and exchanges a look with Kate before turning back to me. "Now it's my turn. Would you happen to have any dirt on a certain illegal gambling ring around town?"

I twist my fingers together on my lap. I knew he would bring it up sometime, and after all he's done for me, I owe him a solid answer. But do I have to incriminate people like Sam, good people caught in a tough spot? And what if Talia happens to be at the races the night the cops bust the operation?

Rhoydes crosses his arms over his chest and murmurs, "I don't need the names of the bikers or the spectators, Taz. The dealers are who we really want."

I let out a big breath and nod. I'm about to tell him what I know, which isn't much, when we're interrupted by the patter of footsteps on the stairs.

"Chase is back," Rhoydes interrupts, shoving his hands into his pockets. "Kate called him after sending me the emails to see if he knew anything about it. She said you two were close and thought you might have let something slip. Naturally, he insisted on coming along and waiting for any news here with Kate."

"Talking about me?" Chase asks, shutting the lounge door behind him. His gaze settles on me, a mixture of concern and hope. I've seen that look before.

A pair of light gray eyes. For some reason, those eyes look familiar...a mix of concern and something unreadable...a long, dark ponytail with hot pink tips streams out behind her helmet...he pulls a string over the top of his shirt and holds it in his palm. There's a bright pink cross dangling at the end… "Pink was her favourite colour."

Suddenly, it all makes sense. I jump to my feet, and Rhoydes immediately stands in front of the door.

"There's someone I need to talk to," I say urgently. Someone who needs to hear about grace and hope and forgiveness. Kate and Chase are staring at me, confused, but there's a look of understanding in Officer Rhoydes' eyes, and he nods.

"Alright, But I'm driving you."

"I'm coming, too," Kate announces behind me, and Chase chimes in after her.

I cast a desperate look at Rhoydes and muster up a smile.

"Th-this is kind o-of something I n-n-need to do alone," I stammer, giving Rhoydes a pleading look. *Get me out of this.*

"I'll take her. It'll be fine. You two stay here," he states firmly, and although confused, the two sit back down again.

I follow the officer out to the cruiser again, and strap in. He slides in behind the wheel and heads out the driveway.

"Head left towards Staten," I say, and he nods.

"1510 Misty Lane?" he asks.

"How'd you know that?" I sputter in surprise.

"I saw on her license," he chuckles, "and I figured that's where you're going. I saw your expression when you made the connection."

"So…you knew?" I thought the puzzle pieces were all in place, but more keep cropping up along the edges.

"I knew as soon as she took that helmet off. I grew up around here, you know. She was a grade behind me in school, my next-door neighbour, and at a lot of the same places I was. To answer your next question, no, I didn't know she was living around here until today. Or that she'd changed her name."

"But when you saw the license, you said-"

"I figured that was something you need to figure out on your own," Rhoydes interrupts.

Traffic is still light this early in the morning, so we make it to Staten in good time. Rhoydes pulls over beside the road at the end of her lane and lets me out.

"I'll stay here. Yell if you need me," he calls before I shut the door. I roll my eyes. Why would I need *him*?

The lights in the shop are on as I approach, and the big overhead door is open. Sam is on her back beside her dirt bike, a wrench in one hand and a pair of pliers in the other. She glances my way before focusing back on the frame of the bike.

"Hey." I stuff my hands in my pockets and lean against the frame of the overhead door.

"Hey," she mutters back, tightening a bolt. Her pink and black jacket is tossed off to the side, and the sleeves of her T-shirt are rolled up to the elbows.

"What are you doing up this late?" I ask curiously.

"Worked the night shift for three years at a diner in Des Moines. Kind of got used to the hours. It's more peaceful at night, you know?"

Easier to hide, I add silently.

"It's a good life. I make enough to live on during the biking season, sometimes touring across the state, otherwise staying around here. I don't need much, and this suits me."

"They might get shut down," I say, feeling compelled to warn her.

She nods and picks up a canister of WD-40. "I figured it was coming," she answers. "I have more skills than just riding a bike."

We're silent for a moment, save for the creaking of her wrench on a stubborn bolt, until I decide to drop the bombshell. "I was talking to your brother," I start, and her head jerks up.

"You were what? He doesn't know I'm here, does he?" she asks, eyes wide.

I shake my head. "He misses you, though."

Sam sighs and rolls into a sitting position, elbows on knees, and stares out at nothing. "They don't know what I've all done, where I've all been. I said I was never coming back. I didn't want them. After all I've said and done to hurt them, why would they want me anymore?" Her voice is filled with despair and longing and two words: if only.

I shuffle my feet and take a deep breath. "Probably for the same reasons I'm not headed to locked doors and steel bars. Sometimes the people we hurt the most show us the most grace and love."

I can't believe these words are coming from my mouth. A few hours ago, I wouldn't have listened to them myself. I walk over and sit cross legged on the cement across from Sam.

This could take awhile, but I have a story to tell, about abandonment, loneliness, and ultimately, being found.

* * *

The bright green leaves sparkle as they flutter in the breeze. A small shower last night left everything looking fresh and smelling like Kate's favourite room spray, *Wildflower Fields,* and the sunshine sets every leftover droplet alight with a rainbow of colour. I lean against the porch railing and close my eyes as the warmth of early summer washes over me.

I never thought life could be this good. It's been two weeks since I tried to escape Oakville on the back of a motorcycle, and those two weeks changed everything. AJ made it into a halfway house, and Jack is tucked away at Camp Serenity until further notice. Sam hasn't contacted her family yet, but she's getting there. As for me and Kate- well, those are her footsteps coming up behind me now.

She places her hands on my shoulders and rubs in small circles. I lean into her, and she rests her chin on the top of my head.

"Do you like Oakville yet?" she asks.

"What made you think I ever didn't like this place?" I tease.

She laughs. "Well…let's just say there were signs. Lots of them." She pauses her gentle massage and moves beside me. "I love you, Taz. I'm not going to let you go." She gives me a squeeze, and I hug her back.

"I know. And I finally believe you."

We don't say much else, because we don't need to. Besides, if there were any more cute sayings or tears, it would be too mushy for both of us.

We're standing like that, side-by-side and arm-in-arm, when a dark gray Honda Civic pulls in the lane and slows to a stop in front of us. Chase and his younger siblings pile out of the car, followed by a slower, more sedate Madame Lemair.

"I forgot to tell you they were coming over," Kate apologizes. "Parker finished his latest painting late yesterday afternoon, and he's eager to show us.

Parker skips up the steps to the porch and grabs my hand.

"Come," he invites softly.

We follow the young boy into the house and up the stairs to the attic. Chase is right behind me, with Kate and Rainey in the middle, and Madame Lemair bringing up the rear.

"Parker is so excited to show you this painting. He wouldn't even let me watch him finish it." Madame huffs as she struggles to push herself up two flights of stairs. "He's been working on it for the last two weeks."

A white sheet is draped over Parker's latest painting. He stands beside it and holds out his hand toward me.

"Taz, you pull it off," he instructs, a wide grin on his face.

I step forward, honoured to be chosen for such a monumental task, and slowly pull the sheet off. I let it fall to the floor as Madame Lemair and Kate gasp simultaneously.

A large, glowing figure takes center stage, His face a familiar rendition of the typical Bible story book Jesus. He has his arms wrapped around half a dozen people.

I examine the people more closely. There's a dark-headed woman in overalls and rubber boots, a round figure in blue with a distinctly French beret on her head, a tall boy with wavy, dark blonde hair, and yes, there in the center, a brown-haired girl dressed in all black, standing between Chase and the smaller figure of the painter himself.

Rainey is the first one to break the silence. "Look! There's me!" she cries, pointing to a golden head of wavy hair at the end of the line, her face resting against the arm of Jesus. "And look! That's you guys!" she adds, sweeping her arm to include all of us.

Parker somehow managed to paint Jesus' eyes in a way that makes Him appear to be looking at all of us, yet at each person individually. It's Parker's best painting yet.

Chase steps up beside me and slips his hand into mine until we catch Kate watching us with a knowing look. Parker looks up and grins at me.

"I call this one *Belonging*."

ACKNOWLEDGEMENTS

I would like to express my deepest gratitude to my family for their support, from reading the (very) rough draft to cheering me on through the publishing process. Especially my sister- for keeping all those sneak peeks and inside tidbits a secret!

A special thanks to my editor, Stephanie, for your patience and careful eye as you made this story better. Your insights and comments were so encouraging and brought out the best in both me and the book.

Heartfelt thanks to my street team, my Instagram followers, and everyone else who helped spread the word and cheered me on along this journey. You made the whole process more exciting!

This book would not be the same without the exceptional cover design by Steve. His creativity and talent brought my ideas to life, and his designs add character and life to the book.

To the readers who join me on this adventure, thank you for giving a place in your imagination for these characters and their journeys.

Finally, a million thanks to the Author of all. You have been with me every step of the way, and You will never leave me nor forsake me.

MORE FROM TORI:

Twin sisters, a forgotten diary,
and the best summer yet-

THE SUMMER OF US

Available on Amazon and Barnes & Noble